MY LIFE ON TV

MY LIFE ON TV

Kimberly Greene

USBORNE

To the men in my life: GLW, TG, JDG and GLG –
more love to each of you than there are stars in the sky,
fish in the sea, and fountain pens at a Bar Mitzvah.

To Nini: Gracias mucho mucho with chocolate and a cherry on top!

To My Coffee Bean Family: You all have no idea how much your
friendship and genuine care (and wicked lattes) mean to me.

To Red: I miss you.

First published in the UK in 2010 by Usborne Publishing Ltd., Usborne
House, 83-85 Saffron Hill, London EC1N 8RT, England. www.usborne.com

Copyright © Kimberly Greene, 2010.

The right of Kimberly Greene to be identified as the author
of this work has been asserted by her in accordance with the
Copyright, Designs and Patents Act, 1988.

Cover illustration by Rui Ricardo for folioart.co.uk.

The name Usborne and the devices ♀ ⊕ are Trade Marks of
Usborne Publishing Ltd.

A CIP catalogue record for this book is available from
the British Library.

UK ISBN 9781409508298 First published in America in 2010. AE
American ISBN 9780794529017 JFMAMJJAS ND/10 01437/2
Printed in Yeovil, Somerset, UK.

CHAPTER 1

Click click click, clack clack click.

Welcome to what *could* be my very last blog post as the little sister of the world's #1 pop star!

Today, my sister, Danni, is making *what might* be her very last public appearance and then *possibly* hanging up her microphone forever – *maybe*.

Confused? Welcome to my life!

Sam stopped typing. She feared that her rush to get

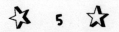

out the trillions of thoughts in her brain would turn her blog into a confusing mess.

Before I tell you what's going on *right now*, I owe you an explanation for not having posted anything on this here blog for the last several weeks. I know it's not fair to go silent like that. *Please* accept this apology, oh faithful blog readers – or faithful blog *reader* (my BFF Olga is the only person I know for sure has read everything I post here) – I promise never to vanish like that again.

See, my summer has been *so painfully* dull that not even a writer as creative as me could come up with anything worth reading. I know that must sound funny considering my sister is a world-famous pop star and I'm living in a mansion filled with hidden cameras and microphones – because my family is starring in a reality TV show – but *it's the truth*! I guess I've gotten so used to all the reality show freakiness that to me it's just a normal part of life. Mind you – "gotten used to it" is not the same as "*okay with it.*" Here's a

painful example of why I'll NEVER be okay with it:

Two weeks ago I got my first zit (groan!), so Mom took me to the drugstore to buy some zit cream. As if having our family's trusty video crew (Michi and Lou) filming the whole trip up and down the zit cream aisle wasn't horrifying enough, the following week, the episode of our show was *ALL* about that first zit (thanks a lot for that, *Mr. TV Director*), and *everywhere* I went random people ran over to tell me THEIR secrets for fighting pimples. URGH!!!

Sam slid her hand around a pile of books on her desk and carefully pulled out a can of orange cream soda. She opened it gingerly to hide the "psst" sound.

Shh! I'm sneaking a can of my fave orange cream soda. Why the drama? Two years ago, after enjoying my beloved orange yumminess, I *accidently* burped on live TV and *to this day* my mom still freaks over anything carbonated. (sigh)

That's just one example of the insanity I deal with daily because of us living in this reality TV fishbowl. When *everyone* can see how you act every minute of every day you have to be superhuman careful not to embarrass your family (or yourself). I try so hard, but I always end up doing something that causes Mom (so she says) to spend so much money on wrinkle cream.

Taking a delicious slurp, Sam licked her lips before setting down the can and returning to her typing.

Olga, my best friend – *now* and *always* – has been visiting family in Mexico, *since May*, while her dad, a famous TV director, has been shooting a movie there. I've been desperately waiting for her to return, but the shoot has taken longer than expected and her trip home has been postponed a million times. Here it is, the beginning of September and still no Olga.

I'm beginning to worry that she won't be back in time for the start of school and this year is

MAJOR! I'm going to Middle School! I don't know about your school, but here, this is when all the cool stuff finally happens like:

- working on the school newspaper
- yearbook staff
- dances

I admit that I'm *so* not a dancer, but the thought of going to a school dance isn't *completely* distasteful. See, I'm going to be fourteen pretty soon and, if you remember from back when I started this blog, one of my fave books is *The Diary of Anne Frank*; I can't get it out of my head that when Anne was fourteen, she wrote about boys and being in love for the first time and kissing and such. Here I am, getting close to that age; how could I *not* wonder if my first love is out there somewhere (like at a school dance) waiting to give me my first kiss? All the other books I read seem to be dealing with this issue when the heroine turns fourteen. So it's totally normal to be thinking about this now, right?

Enough on that – let's focus on my crazy life *now* rather than wondering about my crazy life that *might be*.

With Olga and Danni away, I've been very alone. Now you understand why I haven't written all summer. At least, I hope you do, because finally I'm at a point where I can explain why today MIGHT (or MIGHT NOT) be my sister's final public appearance as a pop star.

It started when Danni finished her latest tour and came home a couple of weeks ago. I had been seriously looking forward to us hanging out and having fun, but *no*, Danni's been nothing but sulky and cranky since she walked in the door. Anything I suggested, she threw back her head and whined, "I'm too tired," "I need some me time," or "don't enter my room without knocking" (she did have a point with that last one). I tried to get her to play *one* video game with me and she pitched a super tantrum (okay, asking an exhausted pop star to play *Rock Band* wasn't my brightest moment — but still — *overreaction*!!)

Danni's mega-annoying mega-successful music agent, Mr. Robert "I'm More Important Than You" Ruebens, majorly got on my case about bothering my sister; he told me to *buzz off* so she could get some rest. Can you believe the nerve of that guy? He doesn't live here (although he's around all the time and helps himself to any food in our kitchen without asking — grrr). He's not a member of our family! What right does he have to say anything about how any of us deal with each other? I *shouldn't* have been surprised, the guy has NEVER been nice to me, but it had started to feel that at least he wasn't being *so* openly rotten about my existence anymore, and he'd stopped giving my mom brochures on boarding schools (I made that last part up — but it's funny, yeah? Maybe someday I'll be a comedy writer along with being a serious author). Mom glared at him with her killer eyeball beams of death (you do not *ever* want to be on the receiving end of that look) and told him to keep out of our family business. Even so, Mom did ask me to give Danni "more space" – which made me roll my eyes because our house is *huge*; you could yell at one end of it and run down to the other to hear the echo. Trust me, you want space, come to our house.

Even with me giving Danni tons of space, she's stayed in her horrible, sullen mood. To some of you, this may not seem like *that* big a deal, but you have to understand, my sister has always been a major part of my life.

When we were growing up, Danni and me didn't have our dad (he died before I was born), any money (Mom was always stressed) or many friends apart from each other (we lived on an army base where the other kids were always coming and going). Things only really changed about three years ago when Danni signed with rotten Robert. She's been crazy busy ever since – and while her success has changed our lives in so many great ways (Mom never worrying about paying rent has been a HUGE relief), I've had to make a massive effort to deal with all the bad stuff (Danni being away on tour and Mom not available because she's dealing with Danni's career). I've been telling myself that this extended rotten mood of Danni's is a temporary thing, but it's getting harder to deal with.

Before becoming a pop star, my sister was always bubbly and a hoot to be around. The Danni I grew up with is sweet, kind, and can make me laugh so hard I almost wet my pants, but as I mentioned, lately she's been a walking bottle of *whine*. If I had a bigger family, maybe it wouldn't be such a big deal — but our family is tiny! I told you about us not having a dad. My Grandpa Abe lives in England, so I don't get to see him much — and anyway, we only met him last year. My mom's parents booted her out when she was a teenager — so I don't know them at all. My mom, Rose, is awesome, but with Danni being a global phenomenon, Mom, as Danni's manager, is *totally about* Danni's career 24/7. And me – I'm into horses, reading and writing (and trying not to cause too many reasons for public apologies).

Sam took a moment to reread all that she'd just written and thought, *Compared to all our nice, normal neighbors, we must seem like a bunch of bananas. But we aren't weird or anything, we're just a bit eccentric.*

Before last Friday, my life had become a decent – if dull – routine of riding at the SuAn stables, reading in my room, and surfing the web (I found a stash of old Sesame Street videos and spent more time with Kermit and Cookie Monster than I ever did as a kid, and – I probably shouldn't admit this but – those Muppets are *really* funny!)

Everything changed last week when I was reading in my room and somebody screamed a huge, hairy, "AURGH!"

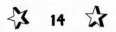

Long story short — Danni had just gotten a voicemail from a dear fan/friend telling her how sad she was that Danni had turned down her formal invitation to appear at a special charity event. Danni went *major firecrackers* because she'd never *received* any such invitation, let alone turned it down.

Sam put her hands over her mouth to stifle the giggles as she remembered her sister yelling at Robert once it came out that *he'd* snagged the invite and sent a "sorry, but no" response without ever telling Danni. Only Rose had ever gotten away with bawling out Mr. Robert Ruebens, so seeing Danni do it was a moment Sam wouldn't easily forget.

Still, Sam had to give the guy credit; he'd kept his cool as he'd explained to Danni, "You get a hundred such requests every day. There's no way you can respond to them all, so yes — I intercepted the invitation. I have people on my payroll who deal with this kind of fan mail, but don't worry, the girl got a personalized autographed picture of you to hang on her wall."

Danni had asked, "*How* could this girl have received

a personalized autographed picture of me that I didn't autograph personally?"

"Oh, Danni," Robert replied way-too-sweetly, "don't you remember? We had you write your name on an electronic tablet with a special pen over a year ago? I explained then that this would allow us to digitize and reprint your signature any time; we did this so you wouldn't hurt your wrist signing letters and pictures day and night."

Sam remembered the scene being interrupted by running footsteps as Michi and Lou, the family's camera crew, came scurrying over. Michi had stopped and focused her video camera a good distance away from everyone, but Lou got closer, and stuck his boom – that microphone on the end of a long pole – directly in between Robert and Danni. None of these intrusions had ever bothered Danni before, but for some reason, that day, it seemed to annoy her – *big time*. She'd actually glared at Michi and Lou! Then, with both hands clenched, she'd returned her angry scowl to Robert and spoken in that same low, slow, spooky voice Rose used whenever one of the girls had gone too far.

"Putting my name on some generic 'thanks for writing' letter is not the same as using a computer to sign a *personalized, autographed* photo." She turned to Rose, "Mom, Robert snagged a letter from Rowan Brown, that very special little girl I met on the airplane last year when we went to meet Grandpa Abe. Remember, I told you about her?"

Rose nodded. "I do remember, darlin', but you can't be too upset with Robert. This sounds like an honest mistake. Part of Robert's job as your agent, and mine as your manager, is to protect you from the millions of demands that come along with being a star. He didn't do anything to hurt you."

"But he did!" Danni wailed.

Cringing at the painful memory, Sam returned to her typing.

I tried to be a good sister and told Danni how bad I felt about her being so upset. I asked when the event had been and she handed me the phone saying she was so *distraught* (a big word for my *not-a-brain-surgeon* sister) that she hadn't paid attention to that. I listened to the voicemail and realized that the charity thing hadn't happened yet! It was still a week away. Danni totally had time to demand Robert clear her schedule and tell the organizers of the charity that she'd love to appear at the event! This was great news – Danni was all happy and that made me all happy. Mom and Robert, however, stayed rather quiet until I asked why neither one of them seemed very excited about this.

Turns out Mom and Robert were in final negotiations with this new company, Dazy Guitars, to sponsor a huge and amazing fall tour for Danni to Toronto, New York, Mexico City, London, Paris, Tokyo, and Sydney. It would be a *Best of Danni Devine Tour* – so Danni wouldn't have to learn any new dances, she could simply do her favorite ones from her previous tours. However, one important part of the deal was that Danni would play a couple of songs on their flashy, pink guitar during the concert. And she needed all the time she could get to practice.

There was a weird moment of silence. It looked to me as if Danni was seriously considering the idea, but then my sister lost it, *BIG TIME*! Right then and there, she told Mom that she was no longer her manager and screamed at Robert that she was done with him and music! Then, Danni looked straight into Michi's camera lens and shouted, "I quit! No more singing! No more dancing! No more reality show! You all can just wave buh-bye to this pop star because she has left the business!"

Yup – it was one U-G-L-Y moment.

And it's been F-U-N-K-Y in this house ever since.

It hasn't *seemed* as if anyone believed Danni was serious about quitting. Robert's continued doing his job; he arranged for Danni to be at the charity thing today (more on that soon) and I've heard him discussing the dates for the fall tour. Mom keeps on performing all her duties as Danni's manager.

And Danni? (Now you'll understand why I'm so confused about whether or not today really is the end of Danni's showbiz career.)

Three times this week a guy has come over to the house to give Danni private guitar lessons (and as a person who has overheard these lessons, let me tell you, it's rather painful). I've been watching Danni very carefully (from a distance mind you – can't afford to get in her *space*) and even though she *appears* to be getting ready for another tour, it's as if she's going through the motions without caring one lick what happens. So…*is* today really her last public appearance or *is* she going to do the guitar tour in the fall??

Your guess is as good as mine. It *seems* like Danni is kind of, sort of, getting ready to go out on this new tour; she hasn't said another word about *not* performing since last week, but then again, she hasn't said that she is going back out on the road. Do three sad little guitar lessons add up to a world tour? I have NO idea, but I'm dying for someone to say something one way or the other and make it official.

Either way, the charity event that caused all the fuss is today, and *finally* I have something truly exciting to tell you!

The charity thing, it's *a horse-riding program* for disabled kids, called *STARS*. Horses – HOORAY! My whole afternoon will be hanging out with Danni and Mom at this wicked party at a huge ranch where I'll get to see a whole bunch of amazing horses that help kids feel better about themselves and their abilities. Could anything be more awesome than that?!?!?

Right now we're all getting ready to go to the big event – and, as I said before, no one really knows if this is the final appearance of Danni as a world-famous pop star or not. It might be – but it might not be. (Like I said, welcome to my life. Nutty, eh?)

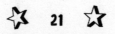

And here I sit, typing away, feeling a million things at once. My gut tells me that Danni would regret giving up being a pop star, but (*confession alert*) I'd be *thrilled* to have my sister bail on showbiz so we could spend time together like we used to.

Sam stopped typing again to take another swig of soda. She glanced around her bedroom. It alone was bigger than the apartment the Devine family had lived in before Danni signed the contract for the reality show and they had moved into the giant mansion. Rose dearly loved this place, but to Sam it had always been completely insane. Why would a mom and two daughters need more bedrooms and bathrooms than most hotels, a kitchen big enough for a restaurant, and a formal dining room so long you could play a full game of field hockey without ever hitting a wall?

I wonder, if Danni *does* quit performing, where will we live? We won't be able to stay in this house — the production company owns it so we're only here while they film our reality show. And while *I* think this place is ridiculous, my mom loves it! She cut a deal with our producers that if we complete three full years of filming, then we *own* this place, but — as of right now — we've only done two years. And seeing as there wouldn't be much of a point in filming a reality show about a pop star's life if there's no pop star anymore then...WHOA! *Would this mean the end of The Devine Life reality show*?

That would be awesome for me! If the show were to end then we would could go back to being normal people!

Hang on, right now I'm totally remembering how hard Mom had to work to take care of us before Danni got all rich and famous.

Okay, now I've got myself tangled in knots. If my sister quits being a pop star, will Mom be forced to go out and find another job so we'll have money for food and a roof over our heads?

Yes, I know lots of money has been made since Danni became a mega-star, but lots of money has been spent, too! You should see the way my mom and sister shop! They drive off empty-handed and come back with their cars so stuffed with boxes and bags that it's a wonder the tires don't burst!

Sneaking another sip of soda, Sam caught sight of herself in the mirror. She focused on her image, but what she was really thinking about was what was behind that mirror. Toying with the possibility of the reality show ending had flashed another worrying vision into her brain. "Blu!" she called out. "Blu! I've got to talk to you!" She leaned over toward a hidden microphone taped to the side of her desk and yelled, "Blu! Blu!"

The enormous mirror covering an entire wall of Sam's bedroom slid out and up, like a garage door. This left a funny blue glare radiating from the big hole where that mirror had been. An astounded voice followed the blue glare out of the giant hole and into Sam's bedroom.

"Have you gone *completely* nuts or is this a momentary loss of volume control?"

Sam half-cringed, half-giggled as she walked over. "Too loud?"

A head full of dreadlocks and two big brown eyes peered out from inside the blue glare. "Loud? You come sit at my desk, wear my headphones, and let me go yell into any one of the hidden microphones all over this house. Then, maybe the world-famous writer-to-be can come up with a better word than *loud* to describe the brain-melting experience you just gave me. Of course," he smirked, "I have only been directing your reality show for about *two years*, so for the past twenty-four months, my crew, with all our state-of-the-art equipment, has captured your every move and sound. Maybe next year, by the time the contract is up and the show is over, you'll finally remember that I hear all, see all and don't respond well to shouting."

"Yeah," Sam looked down at her feet and mumbled. "About that – the show and the contract – I just realized something and really need to talk to you about it."

Blu sat back in his chair. "This sounds rather serious."

"Well, it is." Sam wasn't clear how she was going to ask Blu about the reality show staying on the air if Danni quit or what would happen to their friendship if it ended, but she had to try. "See, you know this afternoon is the charity thing for Danni's friend—"

"The *STARS* event," he interrupted. "Yes I know and I bet I'm even more excited about it than you are!"

Whoa! Sam hadn't expected that. "Why are *you* so happy about it?" she asked.

"How could I not be? *Finally* there's something interesting to video. I mean, no offense, but your lives have gotten rather monotonous. It's not easy to piece together an interesting TV show with the footage we've been getting. For the last episode, the most exciting thing we had to air was you handing Robert the salt instead of the sugar for his coffee."

Sam tried to protest, but Blu cut her off.

"Don't waste my time or your breath telling me again how that was an *accident*. It's over, it's done… and for the record," he leaned closer to Sam, "it was funny."

Dropping her head in mock embarrassment, Sam sat back down and thought about Blu's life as the director of her family's reality show. "I'd never imagined it from your perspective. Boring for me must be seriously dullsville for you, having to watch it every single day. But Danni's tantrum last week and all that about quitting showbiz? That wasn't exciting enough for you? The thought of her career ending and then maybe, probably, this show stopping and you going away and us never getting to talk again, that's not interesting to you?"

Blu pushed his hands out toward Sam. "Hey! Slow down. I'm only looking at this as the director of your reality show. Yes, that dramatic scene with Danni," Blu used his fingers to make air quotes, "'*quitting*' was a good moment for the cameras, but excluding that and this weird week, it's been pretty much boring business as usual."

Sam couldn't believe Blu was so calm about the whole thing. Didn't he care that if the show ended, he'd lose his job and – more importantly – he might never see her again? She'd come to think of him as a big brother; a guy she could always go to for advice and a sense of *it'll-be-okay*, particularly at those times when it felt like it never ever would be.

"So…" she spoke slowly in an effort to seem totally in control and not as crazy-emotional as she really was inside about all this, "help me understand. If Danni *does* quit, that means us Devines go back to being our old off-the-charts boring selves and you'll end the reality show?"

Blu sighed. "Sam, you are thirteen years old. Don't worry so much about tomorrow when you've still got today to deal with."

"But, Blu, this is big stuff," Sam whined. "I'm almost fourteen and this situation has major potential future ramifications on my entire life!"

"Listen up, my friend," Blu leaned forward and replied gently, "I don't have all the answers. I'm ninety-nine percent certain that today *will not* be your sister's last appearance as *Danni Devine, Pop Star*. However, if it is, then we go with it and the changes it'll bring. You know your mom's deal with the TV producers; you don't own this house until you've done the reality show for a full three seasons. As of today, you've only completed two, and if there's no pop star in the family, then I can't stick around to direct a reality show about one, can I?"

Sam was completely tongue-tied by Blu's low-key reaction to this mega world-changing possibility. She jumped up from her chair and threw her hands out in front of her as she stammered, "But...but... but—"

"But right now –" Blu cut her off as he looked over at one of his monitors – "how's about you pull yourself together and go check on your sister?"

Recognizing how her feelings were spinning hot and heavy, Sam drew in a deep breath, held it as she counted to five, exhaled, and then replied softly, "Okay," before walking out of her room. She paused a moment and leaned back in.

"Why should I check on my sister? Do you know something I don't?"

"Sam," Blu said seriously, "you know I can't get involved in your family's lives. I'm not saying anything specific, but I think it would be nice if you went and checked in on your sister before you all go to the party."

With that, the giant mirror lowered down to the

floor. Sam was confused and torn; she wanted to get her blog posted before leaving for the show, but it was really odd for Blu to suggest something like this, so she figured it was worth doing.

Sam reached the doorway to her sister's room, and started running to get enough speed to do a flying leap onto the bed. She was giggling until she looked down and saw that Danni, sitting on the floor and staring at her cell phone, wasn't smiling. Usually, before any kind of public performance, Danni was excited and all into putting on her makeup and fabulous clothes. Right now she just looked sad and weary.

Sam did a somersault off the bed and landed right next to her sister. "Danni! Today is going to be awesome! Why aren't you getting ready?"

With her lower lip quivering, Danni explained, "I did something really stupid. I made a promise I can't keep and I'm going to look like a fool in public." She glanced up at Sam with tears in her eyes. "Other than that, everything is just peachy."

"Aw, Danni." Sam sat up straight to look her sister squarely in the eye. "No one has spent more time in the *looking like a fool in public* department than *me*. Tell me what's going on and let the *expert* in this area see if she can help."

Danni sniffed back her tears. "It's true; you are a walking PR disaster."

With the moment lightened, Sam pushed for info. "Okay, *give*."

Reaching under the bed, Danni pulled out her laptop. She flipped it open, launched a web browser, and pointed to a web page. Once it loaded, Sam saw that it was a big ad for Dazy Guitars. Danni was holding the instrument as if she was playing it. The words, in huge bright text, read: *Danni only does Dazy*.

Sam studied the page. "So?"

Danni pursed her lips. "What does this ad say to you?"

"Umm…" Not sure what she was supposed to be seeing, Sam tried to give the correct answer. "It says you only do Dazy."

Frustrated, Danni pushed further. "But what does it look like to you? What does it make you think?"

Staring harder, Sam replied, "It makes me think you like this guitar."

"You're getting warm. But *who* would like one guitar over another?"

Still not understanding, Sam guessed, "Somebody who plays guitar?"

Danni nodded.

"But," an unsure Sam tried to understand, "you're just learning to play guitar."

"That's right. *I'm just learning*. Keep thinking; you're getting warmer."

The pieces began to fall into place. "So…people who see this ad think you already know how to play guitar because the ad makes it look like you do, but you don't, and that's bad because…" It hit her! "Oh! Someone saw this and thinks you play guitar now and wants you to play guitar at the *STARS* event today!"

"Hot, hot, hot!" Danni cried out as she tapped her nose with her finger. "Rowan called about twenty minutes ago and absolutely begged me to play."

"Come on, Danni," Sam said. "Why didn't you just tell the truth? It isn't *that* big a deal."

"Maybe not to *you*," Danni slammed down the lid of the computer, "but you didn't hear Rowan going on and on about how cool it would be if I would play for her and her friends. I wanted to tell her I couldn't do that, but I couldn't bring myself to when she was so excited." She tugged on her long, blonde hair. "How pathetic would I have looked if I'd admitted that even though I'm this world-famous singer, I know less-than-nothing about music and couldn't play a note on an instrument if my life depended on it? How could this picture be on the web? I haven't even decided if I'm going to support their guitar or do their stupid tour! I didn't pose for that picture! Somebody *Photoshopped* that guitar into my hands; it's a total fake! Just like me – a total fake! You've heard me trying to play – I'm hopeless! I can barely hold a guitar, let alone use it to make music. I can't believe Mom and Robert gave the green light to that ad!" she wailed. "This is too much pressure! I should have said no to Rowan and I need to say no to Mom and Robert, but I don't want to let anyone down. I hate letting people down. I'm such an idiot!"

"Please don't say that," Sam begged. "Everybody makes mistakes. You need to call Rowan and explain that you aren't good enough or confident enough to play in public – *yet*! I know you're trying. I hear you practicing. No, you aren't great today, but if you keep working at it, you will be awesome by the time the tour starts...if you do the tour...which I understand if you don't want to...but either way—" She reached over and held up Danni's phone. "You have to come clean with Rowan. She'll be cool."

Danni sniffed back her tears. "You think?"

Sam nodded furiously. "Oh yeah! Totally! In fact, Rowan will think even *more* of you for taking the time to call her back and share the truth! For reals!"

Despite not being completely confident in the plan, Danni took the phone.

"I'll do it." She began to dial, but stopped. "Thanks, Little Bit. You rock."

Sam beamed with pride, but being called Little Bit tweaked her ear.

"Um, Danni," she whined. "I'm not a little kid anymore; when I was four and pranced around like a pony, calling me *Little Bit* was cute, but seeing as I'm going to be fourteen pretty soon, I'd really appreciate it if you would *please* stop calling me that."

Danni smiled. "Well, I certainly don't want to embarrass you – you do enough of that on your own."

She threw a pillow playfully at Sam. "Tell you what – I promise that I'll work on not calling you *that name* right now, and by the time you do turn fourteen, I'll not only have the problem whipped, but I'll throw you an awesome birthday party. I'll sing *and* play a rendition of 'Happy Birthday' that'll knock your socks off. Sound good?"

Sam grinned and nodded emphatically.

"Good!" Danni nodded back before pointing toward the door. "Now get out of here already so I can call Rowan and get ready for the party!"

Click click click, clack clack click.

Okay, I'm signing off now. As I said at the start of this insanely long post (sorry about that), this *MAY* be my official, absolute last blog as the little sister of a world-famous pop star...and then again...it *MAY NOT*. What will happen? No clue here, but somebody better make a decision soon or the tension is going to make my head explode.

CHAPTER 2

Sitting quietly in the back of the limo on the way to the *STARS* event, Sam got a text message. As she read it, she began babbling excitedly away.

"Mom! Danni! Olga just texted me! She's back! Her whole family got back last night! And guess what? She got all my e-mails and she's coming to the *STARS* event today! I told her all about it and she told her mom and begged and her mom thought it sounded cool – so the whole Victorio family will be there! And she said she has a surprise for me! How awesome is that? We're going to a party at a ranch, my best friend will be there, and she's got a surprise for me! I'm so excited I think I'm going to burst!"

Robert, fiddling with the keys on his Blackberry, spoke without looking at Sam. "When you do, could you try not to get yourself all over my suit?" He glanced up with a pained expression. "Rose, I'm trying to handle last-minute details. Could you please explain to your daughter that it's difficult to conduct business with her unnecessary chatter polluting our shared space?"

Rose patted Sam's knee. "Relax, Little Bit."

Sitting back in her seat, Sam shot a snotty glare at Robert. He saw it and gave her one back. She was about to retaliate with an even snarkier face, when the limo turned into the driveway of a huge ranch, even bigger than the SuAn Stables! It was amazing! Everywhere Sam looked she saw rich, green fields, rolling hills, and horses – lots and lots of beautiful horses!

The limo came to a stop behind a small platform stage. Sam hopped out and marveled at the scene. There were balloons, banners, and wooden picnic tables all around. Even though they'd arrived early, there were already a lot of people there, including a bunch of kids. At first, Sam was surprised to see how many of the children were in wheelchairs or had crutches, but then she remembered the goal of the *STARS* charity and it all made sense.

One pretty young girl wheeled over to Danni.

"I'm so happy you're here!" she shouted joyfully. "All my friends are way excited to meet you!"

Danni bent over and gave the young girl a hug. "Rowan, nothing was going to stop me from supporting my number-one fan."

For a second, Sam was confused. Danni had never said anything about Rowan being in a wheelchair. *Oh*, she realized, *Rowan isn't one of the volunteers, she's one of the STARS kids.* Sam grinned as she watched her sister chat away with the girl, but still, something was off. Danni's smile wasn't as bright as it usually was. *Maybe Rowan was more upset about Danni not playing guitar today than I thought she'd be,* she wondered. *Maybe Danni is going to announce that she's giving up showbiz for real.*

Sam's quiet moment was interrupted by a high-pitched squeal. She grimaced and dropped her head. *Please*, she begged silently, *please don't let it be who I think it is!*

Skinny, bratty, eleven-year-old Inga Victorio waved wildly as she scurried toward Danni as fast as her sparkly, platform cowboy boots and super-tight mini-skirt would let her. "Danni!" she screeched. "Danni, it's me! Danni!"

Sam was torn. If Inga was here, that meant that her big sister, Olga, must be here too, and Sam was dying to see her best friend, but she couldn't subject Danni to Inga's disgusting fawning. Danni was here for Rowan – and if she was already dealing with a case of nerves, adding Inga to the mix could completely ruin the afternoon. She knew what she had to do.

Turning to block Inga's path, she opened her arms wide. "Hellllloooo there, Inga! How are you today? My, it's nice to see you again."

That stopped the charging girl in her tracks. For a second, she appeared surprised, but soon, she returned to her usual snooty pout.

"Hello, Sam," she retorted unenthusiastically. With one hand on her hip and the other playing with the tangle of long chains around her neck, Inga asked, "what do you want?"

Sam acted as if that were the silliest thing she'd

ever heard, "I don't want anything except to talk to you."

"Oh, that's *beyond* not true," Inga sulked. "You're *Olga's* friend. You take *Olga* on cool trips. You don't like me."

"That's not fair, Inga," Sam replied earnestly. "I'm never mean to you. You're the one who makes fun of me. Why don't we at least try to be nice to each other?"

Looking Sam up and down, Inga sniffed, "No can do. As the president of my school's fashion club, I can't be seen *being nice* to somebody who prefers jeans and old T-shirts to designer originals. I have a reputation to protect, you know."

Sam rolled her eyes. "Fine. Don't be nice. Just tell me where your sister is and I'll storm away as if you said something that really insulted me."

Inga brightened up. "That would be awesome! I'd score extra points for cutting down a famous person... well, a sort of famous person...at least, a famous person's sister."

Even though Sam understood that Inga was no more than a spoiled fashion victim, a big part of her really wanted to give this little brat a good talking-to; however, she pulled it together and let Inga's snarky comment slide.

"Okay, Inga," Sam spoke very slowly, "where is your sister?"

"Don't know." Inga shrugged. "She and Dad were coming in a different car. They had to go get – *hey!*" Inga looked around and caught sight of Danni walking toward the stage. "Danni!" She ran around Sam at breakneck speed.

Sam was going to stop her, but she saw a security guard blocking Inga's way, so she didn't feel the need to keep protecting her sister.

Wait a minute! What had Inga said? Olga and her dad were going to get... Get what? Maybe it was Sam's surprise! She wondered what her best friend could have in store for her that was so special she needed her dad's help to get it.

As she thought about this happily, a whole slew of people arrived for the event. Sam had lost track of time, but it felt to her as if, in the blink of an eye, the party had gone from just a handful of bodies to a huge crowd.

"Attention, everyone," a voice called out over the loudspeakers. Sam turned and saw Rowan, center stage, in her wheelchair. She was obviously excited as she waved people to move closer. "Come on over this way! Our program is about to begin!"

Sam weaved her way through the crowd to find a spot where she could clearly see the stage.

"Welcome, everyone, to our *STARS* fundraiser!" Rowan's voice rang out. "As you all know," Rowan continued, "this is the one event where we all get to come together and thank the amazing people who help us kids get to ride, care for and learn all about the great horses they have here."

Rowan asked for the *STARS* volunteers to join her onstage to receive a certificate. Sam smiled and clapped for every person who was singled out.

"Also," Rowan giggled, "let's not forget that this is the one time each year where we get all our friends and family to buy tickets and support our charity financially, so we can keep doing what we love. Usually we offer our supporters a big round of applause as a thank you for this support, but today we have something even more special! Ladies and gentlemen,

I'm super-duper thrilled to get to call onto the stage, my awesome friend, *Danni Devine*!"

Thunderous applause jarred Sam out of her thoughts. She looked up to see Danni walking toward the center of the stage with her "I'm a total pop star" smile; Sam thought her sister seemed more confident and beautiful then ever. *I was silly to worry*, Sam said to herself, *Danni is always happiest when she's performing. It's fun for her to get to sing at such an awesome event as this.*

Danni gave Rowan a peck on the cheek before waving to the crowd and adjusting the mike stand. "Howdy, y'all," she called out. The audience cheered.

"At the urging of a special friend," Danni gave a nod over to Rowan, "I worked up something special for this event. It's an old song, so you know the words, but this will be the first time I've ever been my own band."

Sam shook her head. Whoa! What had Danni just said? Her own band? Robert stepped onto the stage and handed Danni a bright pink guitar, just like the one in that web ad for the fall tour. Sam's heart began racing; her head was swimming so much she stumbled a bit. She looked around to see if anyone else was as surprised about this guitar thing as she was. The crowd was cheering; they didn't know about the conversation Sam had had with Danni that very morning – they didn't know Danni couldn't play her way out of a paper bag! Danni *so* wasn't ready to play in front of people! What in the world was going on here?

Danni looked to the side of the stage and gave Robert a little nod. She counted, "A one and a two and a..." before launching into her song.

Sam bit down hard on her lip and held her breath as Danni's fingers began strumming the guitar. After listening for a minute she was stunned to realize that Danni's playing sounded good – really good! *Wow,* she thought, *Danni's doing great! This sounds hot! How did Danni get so much better since I last heard her?* She relaxed and settled back to enjoy the performance.

At first, Danni stood pretty still while singing and playing, but by the middle of the song, with the audience clapping, singing along and swaying in time to the music, she began to bounce a little. As she sang the chorus over and over, signaling the end of the song was drawing near, she even began to rock out – leaning to the left and the right. This was making for a seriously great guitar-playing debut, until she got carried away and the guitar accidentally hit the mike stand. It wobbled several times before falling over. The thud of the mike hitting the floor was loud, so loud that it spooked everyone – including Danni. She jumped back and threw her hands up to cover her ears.

That move alone was embarrassing, but the truly terrible part was that even though Danni was totally frozen in shock at what had just happened, the sound of guitar playing continued blaring out over the speakers. Sam was confused; if Danni's hands weren't on the guitar anymore, why was the sound of it still coming over the speakers? Then it hit her like a splash of icy water: Danni had been faking! She hadn't been playing the guitar at all! That little nod to Robert must have been a signal to turn on the music so she could act as if she was playing while she sang!

The audience was silent. They, too, took a couple of moments to figure out exactly what was going on. A couple of people booed, some people laughed, but mostly everyone just stared at Danni – waiting to see how she'd deal with the situation.

Danni put her hands over her face and began to cry. The background guitar music finally stopped; the atmosphere was painfully quiet as everyone watched and waited. Sam, knowing how humiliating this had to be for her sister, was dazed and immobile; if anyone had tapped her on the shoulder she'd have gone straight down like a tree in a forest. Danni would never pull a stunt like this! How could it have happened?

Rose hurried onto the stage, put her arm around her daughter, and whispered something into her ear. Danni shook her head and stepped away from her mom. She grabbed the fallen mike, stood it back up, and swallowed hard before speaking.

"I'm sorry. I'm so sorry," she said through her tears. "I shouldn't have…this was wrong…I'm more sorry than you'll ever know. You have every right to be disappointed in me. I was so desperate *not* to disappoint someone," she looked at Rowan, "that I made a terrible decision. Please forgive me."

There was a mixture of "it's okay," "we forgive you," and boos and jeers coming from the audience. Danni waved her hands to get everyone to quieten down. "Please," she begged. "I…I…" Danni put her hand to her heart as if to keep it from jumping out of her body, "I think I need to tell you all that I can't do this anymore." Danni looked up at Rose. "I'm sorry, Mom, I have to say this." She looked back out over the audience. "I'm officially announcing the end of my pop career. I'm hanging up my microphone and retiring."

The audience reacted loudly with displeasure and disappointment, but Danni put out her hands to get them to hush.

"I've been thinking about this for a while and now my decision is made. But, seeing as I owe y'all for what just happened here, I'm willing to try and make it up to you. If there's anyone here who really *can* play guitar, I'd love to sing with them and try to make this last performance one we can all remember for good reasons and not because of my unforgivably stupid and embarrassing behavior. Any takers?"

Sam held her breath. *Please*, she begged silently, *please, somebody help my sister!*

CHAPTER 3

Click click click, clack clack click.

It's five in the evening and I'm back in my room trying to understand how one day could *STINK* so badly!

See, at different times in my life, I've been *annoyed* with my sister, I've been *bothered* by my sister, I've even been hot, spitting *mad at* my sister – but NEVER EVER EVER have I been truly *disappointed* in my sister...before *today* that is.

Danni did something really dumb and dishonest. I'm not going to bother explaining exactly what happened because

#1 – it's too awful to describe, and

#2 – by now it's all over the gossip websites.

Anyway, it almost ruined the whole *STARS* event. Then this super-amazing guy got up onstage, grabbed the guitar, pulled over a stool, sat next to Danni, smiled, and played her three best songs. Just like that! No drama. No big deal. He was like a guardian angel sent to protect her from the disaster she'd created (seriously – he was cute enough to have been an angel). Danni sang her heart out and made up for the whole mess (at least it seemed that way to me).

Now, my sister is an honest person, so I *knew* this couldn't have been her idea. While she was still performing, I looked around for the *rat* – I mean the *person* who *had* to be responsible – *Robert* (grr)!

 49

When I spotted him (hiding behind a giant speaker), my mom was very busy hissing in his ear. I don't know what she was saying, but the guy had a pained expression on his face that made me think he was going to cry! I almost felt bad for him – *almost*.

The minute Danni finished singing, Mom hustled us into the limo. She did this so fast that I lost a shoe. Yup. I tried to explain that *that* was why I kept reaching out of the car door, but my mom was in one of her so-angry-that-she-wouldn't-raise-her-voice-above-a-whisper moods, so my shoe got left behind (bummer – I really liked that pair – they were all broken in and comfy).

Any time anybody started to speak, Mom shot them a ZIP IT glare – it was one long limo ride home. Once we got back here, I realized I never did get to see Olga.
8-(

I ran up here to my room and pounded on the

mirror to talk to Blu, but he didn't answer — it killed me not to be able to talk him when I'm in major crisis mode. (deep sigh)

So now, I'm alone in my room feeling so many different things that I'm seriously light-headed. What do I say to my sister? Whenever *I* mess up big time, I say I'm sorry and do whatever I can to make up for my boneheaded action. It's not that easy here; what Danni did wasn't just some doofy mistake. My sister made a conscious decision to flat-out fool people — including me and Mom — and that's so uncool that I'm not sure it's forgivable.

A knock at Sam's bedroom door startled her.

"Yikes!" she exclaimed.

Olga popped her head in. "Sorry to frighten you. Got a minute for a visit?"

Sam raced over to give her best friend a hug. "Tell me everything!" she demanded, flopping down on the floor and leaning against her bed. As Olga walked over and sat next to her, Sam peppered her with questions.

"Where have you been all day? Were you at the event? Did you know what happened? Why was Inga there before you? How was Mexico? What did you and your dad have to go get?"

Olga tried to answer each question as quickly as Sam spat them out. "I've been trying to track you down. Yes, I was at the party and saw the disaster. Inga and Mom took a separate car. Mexico was fun, and my dad and I had to go back to the airport to pick up—" She stopped to catch her breath. "That's tough! How do you get so many words out with a single breath?"

"It's a gift," Sam giggled.

An awkward silence filled the room as the silliness and excitement of the reunion settled down and the reality of the mortifying scene with Danni came back to them.

Olga dipped her head as she quietly asked, "You didn't know anything about what Danni was doing, right?"

Sam shook her head emphatically. "If I'd had even the *tiniest* clue, I'd have done everything I could to stop that train wreck." She sighed. "What was my sister thinking?"

"I can't imagine," Olga replied. "It's so not cool to try and fool your fans. She had to know there'd be somebody in the audience who'd notice her fingers weren't matching up to the music. You can't get away with that kind of stuff today; the minute a famous person does anything stupid it ends up on some video site for everyone to study and dissect. Even if she'd pulled it off today, she'd have gotten creamed eventually. It's like that old saying: you can fool some of the people some of the time, but you can't fool all of the people all of the time. Who said that?"

Sam thought hard before answering, "Kermit the Frog?"

Olga contemplated this response for a moment before cracking up. "Kermit the Frog?" She stood as she continued, giggling, "That's a good one; I actually thought you were serious for a second. Boy, I missed you this summer. *Kermit the Frog.*" She walked over to the door. "You always have something funny to say when things get too serious." Olga motioned for Sam to follow her. "Come on, I think my big surprise may have the real answer."

Sam pretended to laugh along, but she hadn't

intended her answer to be entertaining; she truly thought it could have been the wisest of the Muppets who said something so smart. She was kind of embarrassed that Olga had found the idea so entertaining. Still, if you're going to say something unintentionally goofy, better to do it in front of your best friend, who'll think it's funny, than say it in front of someone who would rip on you for it.

Completely engrossed in her own thoughts, Sam absent-mindedly followed Olga down the stairs and into the family room.

"Yo," Olga called out as she entered the room and leaned against the back of the sofa, "who said, *you can fool some of the people some of the time, but you can't fool all of the people all of the time*?"

"Abraham Lincoln," an unfamiliar voice answered back. "Those words aren't *exactly* right, but you're close enough to get away with calling it the Lincoln quote."

Looking up, Sam was stunned to see that the question answerer was the super-cool guy who'd played guitar for Danni at the event. *Wow!* Sam thought. *This guy is cute, plays the guitar super-well, is totally smart, and is in my living room!* She was so stunned that she forgot to stop walking and smashed into Olga – hard.

"Ow!" Olga turned around and looked at Sam as if she'd gone totally nuts.

Sam, however, had her eyes glued to the super-cool guy. What was he doing in her house? Was he here with Olga?

Rubbing her now sore shoulder, Olga did the introductions. "Sam, this is Carlos, my cousin from Mexico. Carlos, this is my best friend, Sam."

Carlos gave Sam a warm smile. "Hello."

Sam took a moment to recognize that the super-cool guy was looking at and talking to her. "Uh, hi."

"You have an amazing home." Carlos pointed toward the backyard. "I love that giant pool. Are you a big swimmer?"

"Uh, no."

A strangling stillness filled the room. Sam felt like she should say *something*, but her mind was big-time blanking.

"I don't...don't swim...not as much as I'd like to." She heard herself and thought she sounded like a total doorknob. "I like to swim. I'd like to swim more. I dunk my feet a lot."

Carlos didn't seem to notice anything was wrong. He walked over to the window and looked outside at the beautiful grounds and huge pool. Olga, on the other hand, gave Sam a *what's-the-matter-with-you* look. Sam pretended not to see it and tried to speak like a normal person.

"It's a great pool. It came with the house."

It came with the house? What kind of dumb comment was that? Why couldn't Sam sound even the slightest bit intelligent?

She tried again. "I like to go and sit on the edge and dangle my feet. I should swim more, though. That would be a great thing to do."

Danni walked in carrying a huge ice-cream sundae.

"Carlos," she said with a weary smile, not caring that her teeth were covered in dark, gooey fudge. "I'm glad you came over. I owe you huge."

Had Carlos come over to the house because Danni had invited him? And if so, why did that tweak Sam?

Danni slapped the cushion next to her as she flopped down onto the sofa, put her feet up on the coffee table, and scarfed down a disgustingly massive spoonful of sundae. "Carlos, sit over here and tell me about yourself. How long will you be staying in our fine town, O great guitar hero of mine?"

Why was Danni hogging up Carlos's attention? He was Olga's cousin and Olga was Sam's friend.

"Guitar Hero," Sam chimed in. "That's a great video game! That was funny, Danni. I like to play both Rock Band and Guitar Hero. You play games...video games, I mean, Carlos?"

Olga elbowed Sam and silently mouthed the words, "*You okay?*" as Carlos replied to Sam's question. Sam waved her off and tried to keep an expression of interest on her face as her mind spun round and round trying to think of the next thing to say to Carlos. She wasn't prepared for him to ask her a question – so when she realized there was silence and everyone in the room was staring at her, she understood she'd missed something important.

Danni waved her spoon at Sam. "Hello? Earth to Sam. Carlos asked what other video games you play."

Trying to save face, Sam snapped back at her sister, "I know, I was thinking." Turning her attention to Carlos, she stammered, "Umm...I...I uh, I like...I like the questions, the ones with all the questions. You know, the trivia stuff, the brain-building games."

Danni giggled. "Yeah and we can see how well those brain-building games are working for you right now."

Before Sam could even try to think of a comeback to prove to Carlos she really was an intelligent person, Rose stuck her head through the hatch from the kitchen. "Sam? Oh good, you're out of your room. Hello, Olga. Hello, Carlos. You kids want something sweet? Better get in here fast if you do. Danni's been going after this ice cream like an alley cat in a fish factory."

Sam cringed. *Kids?* Why did her mom have to address them as *kids*? It was obvious that Carlos was at least as old as Sam and Sam was going to be fourteen soon enough!

She looked over at Carlos, who was following Olga into the kitchen. Sam trudged behind, wondering if being called *kids* had bothered him.

As Rose reached into a cabinet and pulled out a couple more bowls, the phone rang. Sam turned to get it, but Robert answered it first. It was bad enough that Robert had come back with them in the limo, but now the big rat was acting as if he was the man of the house!

Sam glowered. Robert pretended not to notice, but it was clear that he had as he handed the phone to Rose and said, "It's for *Mrs.* Devine."

Rose handed the bowls to Olga, took the handset from Robert, and left the room.

Sam wanted to ask Carlos a million questions, but she couldn't find her voice. Her tongue felt like a dead weight, so she stood there, quiet, uncomfortable, and seriously self-conscious.

"So, Carlo," Robert folded his arms. "Where'd you learn to play the guitar so well? That was very impressive what you did today. Ever thought about becoming a musician? You're good enough to do studio work. I could get you a couple of gigs if you're interested."

Sam was both relieved and horrified. It was nice that Robert was filling the weird silence of the moment, but did he have to mess up Carlos's name?

"Thank you," Carlos replied, "but guitar is my hobby. I've been playing my whole life. It is something I do for family and friends. I can't imagine doing it for money."

Stepping around Sam, Robert grabbed a spoon and dug into the entire gallon of ice cream. "Well, if you ever change your mind, let me know. You saved us from a terrible situation earlier and I'd like to repay you."

Holding up the ice-cream scoop, Sam cut into the conversation. "Then how about not getting *your* slobber all over *our* ice cream." She took charge of the gallon. "Olga? Carlos? One scoop or two?"

"One, please," Carlos and Olga answered at the same time.

Immediately Olga pointed at Carlos. "Jinx! You can't talk until somebody says your name." She giggled. "Sam, whatever you do, don't say his name."

Nodding, Sam focused all her attention on trying to get the ice cream out of the container, but the scoop was at a bad angle and the ice cream was still frozen hard. She pushed and pushed and pushed and finally got a scoopful. Unfortunately, she had pushed so hard that it went flying out of the container and landed right in the middle of Robert's expensive crimson tie before falling to the floor.

Robert's face turned as red as his tie. He scowled, got a wet paper towel, and tried to dab away the stain. Olga and Carlos both dropped their heads to hide their amusement. Seeing this made Sam want to laugh as well, but that feeling went away when her mom came back into the kitchen and directed everyone to join her in the living room immediately.

Rose sat next to Danni on the sofa, rubbing her forehead with the back of her hand. Sam immediately knew this was something pretty serious; Rose only did that forehead thing when she was genuinely worried or overwhelmed.

"We have many things to discuss about what happened today," she said gently, "and we just got one more that we need to talk about right now. Olga and Carlos, this is a family problem and I don't want to ruin your afternoon with our issues. You are more than welcome to stay, but I completely understand if you'd rather leave."

"Could we wait outside while you talk, Mrs. Devine?" Olga wondered. "I brought Sam something back from Mexico and I'd like to give it to her today."

Rose smiled. "Of course, Olga. You and Carlos go get some ice cream and then make yourselves at home in the backyard. I promise to release Sam from the family meeting as soon as possible."

As her friends walked back into the kitchen, Sam leaned in and snuggled up to her mom. She was grateful that Rose was letting Carlos and Olga hang out.

"So, Mom?" she asked. "What's the issue?"

Steadying herself, Rose explained gently, "The Dazy Guitar company saw a clip of video from today's event and they are not pleased. They are hoping Danni's big announcement about quitting was just a momentary reaction and that she'll issue an immediate retraction otherwise they need to cancel the ad campaign and find another singer for their fall tour." She turned to Danni. "Sweetheart, what in the world were you thinking? You have worked so hard to build a reputation as a great singer and dancer. All you needed was more time to practice and you could indeed have played that guitar for the whole world – but you weren't ready and you knew it. I've tried to raise you girls to always do your best and be good, honest people. Why would you pretend to do something you couldn't…in front of a crowd…at a charity event? I need to understand why you did what you did."

Danni looked so sad that Sam wanted to step in

and say something that would make everything okay, but she couldn't think of anything.

Robert walked to the center of the room. "I'll take the fall," he said. "Blame the whole thing on me. I pushed Danni, even though I knew she wasn't prepared. I thought this would be great PR for the fall tour. I can handle the heat. If I'm the bad guy, then Danni's reputation stays intact and everything will be all right."

"No, Robert." Danni stood up and walked over to the wall that held all her awards and trophies. She leaned against it, and let her head hang down. "This was all me. I've been too fried to learn anything from my guitar teacher and honestly, I never really tried. I pushed Robert to plug my iPod into the speakers rather than the guitar; what you heard was one of the practice tracks my teacher laid down for me." She turned to face everyone. "Look, it boils down to a simple fact; I don't want to do this anymore. I meant what I said last week, I'm hanging up my pop-star crown."

"I hope you realize that quitting show business is a very big deal," Rose said quietly. "Once you retire, other people will race in to take your place. This is a very serious decision that shouldn't be made when you are exhausted and unhappy."

"But, Mom," Danni wailed, "I'm always exhausted and unhappy! I want my life back. I don't want to be the center of attention anymore. I want to step out of the spotlight and just be normal again."

"And your contract with me?" Robert asked. "That means nothing? I've invested a great deal of time and hard work into building your career. If you quit, then what happens to my business? You expect me simply to smile as you break our deal and I lose a load of my own income?"

Danni pulled on her hair as she struggled to answer him. "Look, Robert, I know I owe you huge for everything you've done for me – for my family, but you don't want a client who is miserable. Even if I did manage to pull it together for this fall tour, I'd be awful and people would stop coming to the shows. You have other clients, and you and I both know you'll be able to find the next *me* soon enough. I'm talented, but there are tons of other girls out there who can sing and dance as well as me, and they are dying for you to discover them and let them be the next big thing. I'm fully aware of what I'm saying; I'm over this life and officially done being a pop star."

Sam gulped. This was exactly what she'd tried to discuss with Blu. Danni quitting the music business meant no more reality show…and that meant no more house, no more job for Rose, and no more Blu. She had to find a way to fix this situation.

"Listen, Danni," she chirped, "what if you just took a little time off? We could go on a vacation – not some fancy shmancy resort, but get in the car and go camp out in motels like we used to! Remember how great it was doing all that silly stuff like visiting the world's largest thermometer or getting lost in the Grand Canyon? Remember sleeping in a tent and waking up to everything covered in snow and how we had to huddle in the car in our sleeping bags to get warm? And we were so far out in the middle of nowhere that we couldn't even get a decent radio station so we sang camp songs until the park ranger rescued us? That was hilarious! We need a break from the whole world – no cameras, no microphones, no TV crew taping our every move. We *all* need to be normal again for a while and then when we come back, maybe we could consider some ideas for making this reality show a lot less painful for you and still super-interesting for all our viewers."

"Hey," Robert chimed in. "Nix the talking about the TV show. We are being filmed right now, remember? We cannot talk about the show. We cannot acknowledge it. We must act as if it does not exist."

Sam wanted to come back at Robert with a juicy zinger about how much she wished *he* didn't exist, but being a mature *almost* fourteen year old, she managed to hold her tongue.

Danni sat up and glared at Robert. "But it does exist, Robert." She wiped the tears out of her eyes. "This is insane."

"What's insane?" Sam asked.

"This..." Danni waved her hands in the air, "this whole...*everything*. Living in a house full of cameras and microphones, having a TV crew following us everywhere, trying to pretend I'm *always* happy because a picture of me frowning gets plastered all over the internet with wild rumors of me falling apart. We need to be normal again; I need to be a normal person again, and that can't happen here. I think I need to move out."

Robert and Rose both jumped into action, reeling off reasons why the idea of Danni moving out was wrong, but Danni shook her head and covered her ears.

"Look," she said as she stomped her feet and put her hands on her hips. "I'm eighteen years old. I have plenty of money. I've worked my heart out for the past three years doing everything that was asked of me, but now I'm so busy trying to please everybody that I'm doing really dumb things. Carlos totally saved my skin today, but he shouldn't have had to." She looked over at her mom. "I'm not smart like Sam. It's no secret that I'm not the sharpest knife on the butcher's block, but I know better than to do what I did today. I am totally ashamed of myself."

"Honey, everybody makes mistakes," Rose cooed.

"No, Mom." Danni shook her head again. "I've already told you, this was no mistake. I was trying so hard not to disappoint *any*body that I ended up practically destroying my entire reputation and disappointing *every*body. I bullied Robert into helping me. I'm the bad guy here. I'm the one who should take the heat. And for once, I really am going to be the one who deals with the consequences of my choices and actions. I'm moving out. I'm giving up singing. I'm done being a pop star and all the baloney that comes with it. You need to listen to me and accept what I'm saying because I mean this with all my heart: I'm d-o-n-e, *done*!"

CHAPTER 4

Sam pounded on her bedroom mirror. "Blu! Blu!" She held still as she waited for a response that never came. "Blu? Come on, Blu! BLU!"

A huge, "Shhhhhhhhhhhhhhhhhhhh," filled the room.

"Sorry," Sam whispered. She tapped on the mirror. "Please open up! I really, really, really need to talk to you!"

"You do realize I'm working here?" Even though he spoke softly, Blu's voice still bounced from one end of Sam's bedroom to the other.

"Please open up!" she whined.

He sighed. "Okay, okay. Step back so I can raise the mirror."

Once the entryway between bedroom and the control room was open, Sam hopped in. Her eyes hadn't adjusted to the dark light yet, so she bumped into a table and almost tripped over a cable.

"How do I fix this mess?" she asked breathlessly. "Danni can't move out! She can't leave! What do I do?"

"I don't know, Sam." Blu shook his head. "I don't think there's anything you can or should do."

Sam's eyes bulged out of her head. "You mean you think my sister quitting showbiz and moving out is a *good* idea?"

Leaning back in his chair, Blu put his hands up in front of himself. "Easy. I'm not making *any* judgements on *anything*. I'm very disappointed by what your sister's suggesting, but I respect her for recognizing that she needs to make some changes in her life. I'm simply saying that it takes a big person to admit when things aren't working and be open to doing stuff differently."

"But, Blu," Sam couldn't understand why Blu didn't seem to recognize how serious this was, "with Danni moving out, it's the end of the TV show and Mom and I have to move as well, right?"

Blu nodded.

"And then there's no more Michi the videographer, or Lou the sound guy."

Blu nodded again.

"And that means…" Sam's lower lip began to quiver. "That means there's no more *you*."

Turning his head to look at the wall of monitors, Blu replied softly, "You are correct."

Sam didn't dare speak for fear of crying. She swallowed super-hard to try and dislodge the major lump that had suddenly filled her throat.

"No," she declared as she thumped a fist down on Blu's table. "I can fix this. I can make it all good. I'll find a way to keep us in this house and the show on the air!"

"Hey." Blu pointed to the top right screen on the wall. "Your friends are still waiting for you outside. Why don't you go do some of that famous foot dunking you were rambling on about?"

Oh duh! After Danni's big dramatic scene, Sam had chased her sister up the stairs to talk to her, but Danni had locked herself in her room. Then Sam had rushed right over to talk to Blu, totally forgetting about Olga and Carlos.

Turning to leave, Sam whipped back around and pointed at Blu. "This conversation isn't over."

Blu gave her a serious, "Yes, Ma'am," before returning to his TV monitors.

Sam slipped out of the control room, hopped down the stairs two at a time, and bustled into the backyard where Olga and Carlos were sitting on a large swinging chair.

"Sorry about all that," Sam said as she closed the door behind her. "Want to go sit by the pool?"

"Yes!" Carlos and Olga answered at the same time.

"Jinx!" Carlos yelled. "Now *Olga* can't talk until someone says her name. *Ha!*"

Laughing, his cousin stuck out her tongue. "You just said my name, *chistoso*. And *you're* still jinxed from before."

"What's a cheese toast-o?" Sam asked.

Her question made Olga and Carlos burst out laughing. As the three made their way to the swimming pool, Olga explained that *chistoso* is a Spanish word that means something like *goofus*. They took off their shoes, sat on the ground, and dangled their feet in the lovely warm water of the Devines' pool, while good-naturedly arguing over just exactly who was jinxed, when the jinxes had gone into effect, and other various jinxing rules.

As they relaxed, Olga pulled a small envelope out of her pocket. "I got this for you my very first day in Mexico. Before you open it, I need to explain an old saying my grandmother taught me. It goes, *la amistad es lluvia de flores preciosas.*"

"That's lovely." Sam reached for the envelope, lost her balance, and wavered on the brink of falling into the pool. She threw her weight far enough back to regain her stability and grabbed onto the edge of the pool with all her might.

"I hope those beautiful words aren't anything about being graceful or coordinated," she joked, "because if they are, I really shouldn't touch whatever's in that envelope."

"You are safe," Carlos replied as he took the envelope from Olga and placed it in Sam's hands. "That saying is an old Aztec poem. It means *friendship is like a shower of precious flowers."*

Suddenly, Sam found herself all tongue-tied again. What was it about Carlos that made her brain turn to mush? She managed to nod and whisper, "Thanks," before forcing herself to focus all her attention on the little envelope.

"Oh, Olga!" she exclaimed once she opened it. "This is so cool it's *hot*!"

Sam carefully pulled a small ring out of the envelope and examined it. On top of the thin band was a perfect, silver rose. She slipped it onto the first finger of her right hand. "Wow, it's kind of heavy! I like that. It feels solid. Thanks, Olga."

She was holding up her hand to admire the awesomeness of the ring when a thought struck her. "Wait, you got this your first day in Mexico? But Inga said you had to go to the airport to pick up a surprise or something."

Olga threw her hands out toward Carlos. "Ta da! This is my big *surprise or something*!" She scrunched up her nose at her cousin, who was more than happy to do the same back to her. Smiling, Olga continued, "Carlos is moving in with us so he can graduate from an American high school. Then it'll be easier for him to go to an American college and then onto medical school."

Carlos was going to stay? He was going to be living with Olga? This was amazing! This was horrible! Why was Sam's stomach suddenly doing major back-flips and feeling all queasy and why was she so embarrassed about it? All she could manage to say was, "That's nice," before turning all her attention back to her beautiful ring in an attempt to avoid eye contact with Carlos.

No one spoke for a couple of seconds, but to Sam it felt like an eternity. She was beyond relieved when Olga broke the freaky silence.

"Okay…well, you want to tell us how things went in the big family meeting?" she said with a wry smile. Is Danni in big trouble for what she did…er…tried to do?"

Sighing, Sam shrugged. "Kind of…not really. It's totally…I can't believe I'm saying this." She looked back at the mansion. "For two years now I've been a total goof about trying to get us out of this crazy house and stupid TV show. Now Danni says she's quitting showbiz and moving out." Sam saw Olga's stunned expression. "Yeah, *for real* – you heard her at the party – she just confirmed it with Mom and Robert. And if she goes through with that, then I get my wish about everything being normal again." She dropped her head and swished her feet in the water. "So, how come I'm not feeling better about all this?"

The quiet of the moment was interrupted by Rose's voice ringing out across the backyard from her bedroom balcony. "Sam, it's getting close to supper time. I figure this family could use a home-cooked meal so I'm making my world-famous chili con carne. Would your friends like to join us?"

"Not if they value their digestive tracts they won't," Sam said under her breath. She hadn't meant anyone to hear, but Olga and Carlos both did and each one practically bust a gut laughing.

Smiling, even though she had no idea what was so funny, Rose held her hand up to her ear and waited for an answer.

"Thanks, Mrs. Devine," Olga shouted up once she'd squelched her giggles, "but I promised my mom we'd be home early. Tomorrow is picture day at the stables and she wants to pick out my clothes with me before she and my dad go out for the evening."

"Picture day?" Rose screeched. "The SuAn Stables annual picture day? Samantha Sue Devine! Did you forget to tell me something?"

An anguished groan escaped Sam's lips as she slumped down like a deflated balloon. With her eyes squeezed shut, she tried to respond in a sincere voice, "Sorry, Mom. I completely forgot."

Covertly, she glanced over at Olga who mouthed the words, "*So sorry*," with a pained expression on her face.

Rose had already gone back inside and down the stairs. She was standing over Sam before her daughter could finish trying to tell Olga not to worry about it.

"Picture day is my favorite day of the year!" She gently tapped the top of Sam's head. "I cannot believe you forgot to tell me." Rose clasped her hands and bowed her head to Carlos and Olga. "Thank you both for coming over. I'm sorry you've had to witness so much…family stuff." She nodded at Sam and Olga. "Now, if you will excuse us, I need to take Little Bit upstairs to prepare for tomorrow."

Sam cringed. Could this moment get any worse? First her mom makes a big deal about *picture day*. Then she has to go and call her *Little Bit* – all in front of Carlos.

Luckily, Olga and Carlos were already busy drying off their feet and putting on their shoes, so they didn't seem to notice. Sam walked them both to the front door.

As her friends stepped outside the Devine mansion, Sam tried to say goodbye, but was interrupted by Rose yelling from the kitchen, "Have a good night, kids. See you tomorrow for picture day!"

Olga and Carlos completely cracked up again as Sam gritted her teeth and gave a brusque, brief goodbye wave. She shook her head in utter disbelief that she was going to have to suffer the total mortification that was picture day.

Click click click, clack clack click.

Today has been off-the-charts weird! Danni messes up big time, Olga's cousin rescues her, Danni announces she really is done with pop music AND she's moving out. Robert is not the total bad guy (for once), and Carlos (he's Olga's cousin) is sticking around for a while and this (the part about Carlos) makes me both kind of happy and sort of sick.

Beep! Beep!

The sound of Sam's cell phone ringing in her pocket startled her. Pulling it out to see that Olga was calling put a grin on her face.

"Hey! Long time no see!" Sam joked.

"Yeah, um…" Olga waited a second before asking, "Can you talk?"

"Sure. What's up?"

Olga again hesitated. "Can you *talk* talk?"

"Yes," Sam replied, a little confused. "I'm in my room. Something wrong?"

"I…I don't think so, but…I hope not. I'm wondering…see, it's hard, but…"

"But what?" Sam practically spat. Had she done something awful? Had she hurt her best friend's feelings? What was going on here?

"Okay. Here's the thing…"

Sam waited and waited, but still there was nothing but quiet from Olga's side of the conversation.

"What?" Sam cried out. "What did I do? Are you mad at me?"

"Oh no! I'm not mad at you," Olga replied emphatically. "I'm thinking that you might be mad at me."

"Mad at you?" Sam was astounded. "You're my best friend! Doing nothing with you is *way better* than the best day I could possibly ever have with anybody else!"

"So then," Olga spoke softly, "is it Carlos? Do you not like him?"

Whoa! Not knowing how to answer, Sam tried to deflect. "Umm...why would you ask that? Did I do something mean or stupid?"

"No, no, no, but you weren't very friendly to Carlos."

Sam was flabbergasted. It took all her might to swallow down the lump in her throat and ask, "What do you mean?"

"You know what I mean. Normally, you're super-nice and funny and you talk to everybody. With Carlos, he'd ask a question and you'd give him a one word answer and look away or you'd say something strange and babble on and on, again without looking at him. Did he say something that upset you?"

"No!" Sam shook her head (as if Olga could see this). "No! Carlos didn't say or do anything wrong. I didn't mean to come off so...*bad*. I don't know... every time I tried to talk to him, I feel...it was weird. I couldn't look at him because he made me..."

It was Sam's turn to leave the conversation hanging with an odd silence.

"He made you what?" Olga pressed. "Angry? Unhappy?"

"Nauseous," Sam said quietly.

"Nauseous? My cousin made you sick?"

Sam scrunched up her entire face. "Yeah. Oh, Olga. I'm really sorry if I seemed rude. I think Carlos is awesome! The way he jumped up on the stage and helped Danni – he's so nice and smart. And he's also super—" Sam stopped herself on the verge of saying something wickedly embarrassing.

"Super what?" Olga asked. "Hang on, were you going to say super-*cute*?"

Sam didn't want to answer. "Yeah," she admitted meekly.

Olga exploded, "*I KNEW IT!*"

Sam flew forward in her chair and hunched over to try and muffle the sound of her voice getting picked up by Blu's hidden microphones. "Please," she whispered, "please don't say anything! Please! Please! Please!"

"I knew it! I knew it! Okay, I didn't know it, but I thought – *maybe*! This rocks! This totally rocks! Oh, Sam, this is terrific! No, it's beyond terrific; it's mega-riffic! It's mondo-riffic!"

"It's *mortifying*!" Sam wailed. "Promise me you won't say a word! I'd crumble up and die if he knew. Please, Olga! Please promise me – not a word!"

"But, Sam," Olga argued, "this is a good thing! What could be better than my best friend hooking up with my best cousin? Carlos is all that *and* a bag of chips! He's like my brother. Did you know he wants to be a doctor? What an amazing couple you'd make – the world's greatest doctor *rolling* with the world's best horseback riding writer?"

Dropping her head and groaning, Sam begged, "Stop saying that. I'm not *rolling* with anybody. I don't even know what *rolling* means, but it sounds totally embarrassing."

"It's not embarrassing; it's awesome. It's like dating except that you're not just boyfriend and girlfriend – you're *real* friends. How wicked is that?"

It would have been way wicked except that having her first serious infatuation with a guy was new and potentially humiliating territory. What if Carlos found out she liked him and laughed? What if she and Carlos did begin *rolling* and then had a big fight? Would it ruin her friendship with Olga?

"Just promise me you won't say anything, at least for now, please?"

Olga's voice was very solemn. "I promise."

"Thank you." Sam sighed with relief.

"No probs, but seriously, this is a really good—" A knock on Olga's bedroom door interrupted the conversation. Sam heard her best friend say, "Sure thing, Mom. Hey, Sam, it's dinner time. I have to go. Talk later?"

"Hope so," Sam answered, "but don't forget, now that my mom knows that tomorrow is picture day, the rest of my night may be torturously painful."

Olga groaned. "So sorry! Maybe your mom will be too busy dealing with all the Danni drama to spend too much time with you. It's not as if picture day is that big a deal, right?"

"Maybe not to us," Sam responded slowly, "but for my mom, any chance to get a photo of me all dressed up is practically a national holiday. Any minute now she's going to bust in and order me to try on every single article of clothing I own to find the perfect outfit – which is insane because she hates all my jeans and T-shirts so I'll end up having to wear something she pulls from Danni's closet and then fancies up even more with sequins or feathers."

Olga giggled as she hung up the phone. Sam sat quietly. Okay, the cat was out of the bag, she'd admitted that she liked Carlos. Now what?

She leaped up from her chair and flopped down on the bed. Staring up at the ceiling, her thoughts were spinning so fast that, even though she was lying flat, she still felt dizzy. This was her very first crush. When other girls liked boys, they seemed to change. They would act all silly or get dopey and giggly or dress fancy – stuff Sam thought was seriously dumb. She really needed to talk to somebody. But who could she trust? Her mom would make a big deal out of it and embarrass her; and anyway Sam was currently hiding from Rose. Danni would totally know how to deal with this, but she was dealing with her own drama and Sam feared that going to her sister would make this very personal situation become just another mortifying episode of *The Devine Life*.

"Ah!" Glancing slyly over at the mirror, Sam softly called out, "Blu?"

There was no response.

Scooting over to the edge of the bed, she tried again. "Blu? You around?"

The room reverberated with Blu's hushed voice. "I am, but I'm crazy busy and trying to get out of here."

"Five minutes. Please?" Sam batted her eyelashes and flashed her sweetest smile.

"Give it a rest," Blu answered. "I have four sisters. I'm immune to cuteness."

Sam pursed her lips. Blu was the closest thing she had to a big brother and she needed his perspective on dealing with this new world of *liking a guy*. Normally

Sam would've discussed something this serious with Olga, but seeing as Carlos was her cousin, that didn't seem possible. What was that thing Olga had said about Sam and Carlos *rolling*? Something about it being awesome because a guy and a girl could be *friends* as well as being boyfriend-girlfriend? That idea sounded wonderful, but Sam wasn't sure how that worked in real life.

She walked over to the mirror and raised her hand to tap on it, but before she could, *Hurricane Rose* came busting through Sam's bedroom door full of gusto and excitement, armed with a truckload of fashion magazines.

"It's *let's prepare for picture day* time, Little Bit!" She whirled over to the bed and dropped her bundle of magazines. "The most wonderful time of the year!"

"But Mom," Sam joked, "you've always said Christmas was the most wonderful time of the year."

Rose threw open her daughter's closet doors. "Any time I can get you out of those boring old blue jeans and into something fashionable is a jolly holiday for me." Whipping around toward the door, Rose put her hand up to her mouth, and called out, "Gentlemen! We're ready!"

Jehan and Jean Tissaire, the freakishly identical twins who served diligently as Danni's beloved hair and makeup artists and stylists, bounded into the room. Immediately, the three adults began tearing through Sam's closet like hot knives through butter. Sam slipped down onto the ground next to her bed and toyed with the idea of crawling out of the room, but before she could move a muscle, the mob had turned and began demanding she try on one piece of clothing after another.

It was a very long night.

CHAPTER 5

Sitting in the back of a bright yellow Hummer limousine was a major embarrassment.

Sitting in the back of a bright yellow Hummer limousine *with Robert Ruebens* was a major embarrassment *and* unbearably silent. Sam caught a glimpse of her reflection in the window and shuddered; everything about this day, this outfit, this moment was just wrong, wrong, wrong. The fringy, sequined clothes, the hat with a huge feather, the painfully blow-dried hair, and sparkly makeup (makeup!) that her mom, Jean, and Jehan had forced her to wear made her look like some psycho-disco rodeo clown.

As the limo pulled up to the security gate of the SuAn Stables, Sam began to panic. This was the one place where she didn't feel like a world-class freak. The stables had served as her escape from all the TV/pop-stardom madness that had infected the rest of her world. Showing up in this awful limo, in these ridiculous clothes, with makeup on her face, and having Mr. *Hey-Everybody-Look-At-Super-Important-Me* Robert making a scene every chance he could, might ruin this oasis forever.

"Robert," she said in her most grown-up voice, "what would I have to do to get you to turn this limo around and let us go back home?"

He didn't even bother looking up from his Blackberry. "Let it go, kid. I tried everything I could to get out of this, but your mother is a tough lady when she sets her mind on something – and she *definitely* set her mind on this."

Sam pulled her knees up to sit cross-legged on the seat. "I know, but still, why couldn't *you* have gone house-hunting with Danni and let *Mom* come here with me? Or better yet, why couldn't I have come alone?"

Glancing over, Robert replied flatly, "Apparently your sister is rather *displeased* with me for telling her the truth."

Unsure what that meant, Sam asked, "Huh?"

Robert rolled his eyes as he set down the phone. "I told Danni that her plan to move out of the mansion and give up singing was childish, foolish, and something she'd regret the rest of her life."

Sam pressed for more info. "*You* think Danni will regret quitting? You're actually worried about *her*?"

"Of course I'm worried about her," Robert snapped. "She's sweet and talented, and yes, she's made me a very rich man; I should be looking out for her. I owe her that much at least. I don't want to see her unhappy. She needs a *vacation* – not a one-way ticket to the unemployment line! But does she listen to the man who made her a world-famous pop star? No. Instead she goes running to her mother and cries about *the big bad agent* trying to control her life. Thus now she's out house-hunting with Rose and I'm stuck on picture patrol with you."

"Well," Sam snapped back, "maybe if you hadn't been such a manipulating meatball these past couple of years she'd have listened to you!"

Sam couldn't believe the words had popped out of her mouth like that. Her eyes flew wide open as she waited for Robert's reaction.

He stared at her for a good sixty seconds before responding.

"Did you just call me a *meatball*?" he asked, seeming more surprised than angry.

Folding her arms in front of her, Sam nodded. "I did. What are you going to do about it?" She suddenly realized a way out of this awful situation, "That was terribly rude of me; if I were you, I'd punish me by *turning this limo around and taking me back home this instant!*"

Robert's eyes bored into Sam. He seemed to be studying her, as if she were some alien creature he'd never seen before. She stared back for a couple of seconds, before getting really weirded out by all the eye contact and needing to blink.

"What?" she demanded.

Settling back into his seat, Robert shook his head, "Nothing. I'm simply slightly impressed at how expertly you tried to manipulate me."

A semi-sort of compliment from Robert? This funky day was getting even funkier.

The limo came to a stop next to the Victorio's Porsche. Olga and her mother were standing next to it. Mrs. Victorio was signing autographs for a large group of girls and not looking too happy about it. Olga rushed over to Sam.

"You've got to help my mom! *Please*," she pleaded, "call her over for some problem. Give her a polite excuse to get away from these fans. They're driving her crazy, but she doesn't want to be rude."

Robert stepped out of the limo and yelled, "Giselle! I'm sorry we're late. I've got those important papers for you. Could you come over and sign them immediately?"

Initially startled, Mrs. Victorio turned and gave Robert one of her world famous beautiful model smiles. "Yes, Mr. Ruebens," she shouted back. "Let me sign *just one more* autograph for these lovely fans here and then I'll be right there!"

There was a groan from the crowd, but they still cheered and waved as Mrs. Victorio blew them kisses, then hustled over to the side of the limo with Sam, Olga, and Robert.

"Oh, Mr. Ruebens," she said breathlessly in her cool German accent. "Thank you, thank you, thank you! I do not understand how many people can still want my autograph after I've been modeling for so many years. You'd think people would be bored of me."

"But, Mom," Olga said gently, "you forget that these are kids and they're not into high fashion, they're all big horse fans. When they saw those ads for that wicked new line of riding clothes – that was the first time they'd ever seen you. Please lighten up. This is supposed to be a fun day, remember?"

Something about Olga's statement caused Robert to brighten up and engage in conversation. "World famous Giselle Victorio is modeling for a line of horse-riding clothes?"

Mrs. V laughed. "Yes. It's a lovely line, very chic and rather expensive. I was quite surprised when they approached me to be their model, but apparently horse riding is huge and growing all over the globe, so there is an audience for such things."

"Now that is very interesting." Robert smiled back.

The glare from his way-too-white teeth almost

blinded Sam. *What is he up to?* she wondered. Before she could find out, Olga grabbed her arm and dragged her over to the picture area.

"Carlos is around here somewhere," she whispered in Sam's ear.

Sam's stomach knotted up. "You didn't say anything to him?"

"Of course not! I would never break a promise to you."

Sighing with mega amounts of relief, Sam relaxed – a little. "I look ridiculous, don't I?" she asked.

Olga examined Sam carefully. "Well, the pink feather on your hat is a bit much, but the makeup is awesome. Your eyes have never been such a deep, sparkly green."

"Let me see."

Carlos had walked over while the girls were chatting. He peered down into Sam's eyes. She was so stunned by this that even though she wanted to run and hide, she couldn't move a muscle.

"Wow," he said as he stood back up, "they are greener than yesterday. That's wild how they changed color."

"Yeah, wild, ha ha." Sam tried to laugh off her utter mortification while looking around for some excuse to bolt. In sheer desperation, she waved at Robert.

"Hey, Robert," she yelled with all her might, "it's almost my turn for a picture. Didn't Mom want you to check some stuff?"

Robert was still talking to Mrs. Victorio, but the sound of Sam calling out to him for assistance was so astounding that he excused himself and headed over.

"You bellowed?" he responded dryly.

"Umm…yeah." Sam's focus zipped back and forth from the ground to Robert in an effort not to accidentally make eye contact with Carlos. "I just remembered what Mom said about you making sure everything was good for the picture. Not that I care or anything, but, you know, I wouldn't want Mom to be unhappy with my picture…because she's the one who cares about this stuff, you know, photos and all that."

Glancing up at Olga, Sam saw an expression of pained empathy. *I must sound like a complete doorknob*, she thought. *I have to get a grip. Focus on being Carlos's friend. Don't even think about the girlfriend stuff.*

She forced herself to smile, look directly at Carlos,

and try to appear totally normal. "My mom takes family photographs *very* seriously."

To her delight, Carlos nodded. "I know what you mean. Before my mother passed away, she used to make a big deal out of every chance to take a picture. It used to drive me crazy, but now that she's gone, I see those pictures and remember how happy it made her taking them."

Sam stammered, "I…I didn't know you'd lost your mom. I'm so sorry to hear that. My dad died when I was…um…actually…he died before I was even born."

Carlos nodded again. "I know. Olga told me. I'm sorry for you too. That's one reason I think you are cool; you've had something terrible happen but you don't wear it on your shoulder or use it as an excuse to be angry or depressed all the time."

Suddenly, the spinning-around Sam had been feeling moved from her stomach to her head. She and Carlos had something in common – yes, it was something sad – but still, they had common ground. This could be the super key to building a friendship. Plus, had he just said he thought she was cool? He said it was *one* reason why he thought she was cool; so there were other reasons too! Could that mean that he liked her? And if it did – did he *like* her like her – as more than just a friend – as a hanging together kind of girlfriend, or did he...

Robert's loud voice jarred her out of her thoughts. "Hello? We're not going to wait all day."

Turning, Sam saw Robert standing next to the photographer and the big bale of hay she was supposed to sit on for the picture. Even though his expression was one of extreme annoyance, he looked so totally out of place, with his fancy business suit and tie in a sea of people in their best riding gear, that Sam couldn't help but let out a tiny giggle.

Catching her laughing at him, Robert quietly snapped, "Find something entertaining?"

Sam, busy adjusting her hat as she strode across to sit down on the hay, couldn't stop herself from answering, "As a matter of fact, I do."

Surprised at her response, Robert replied earnestly, "I'm sure whatever it is it's at my expense, and if so, you'd better enjoy it while you can. As soon as we complete all the paperwork to end your sister's contract with me, I'm gone."

As she tried to smile and follow the photographer's directions, she realized that all the changes happening meant not only losing Michi, Lou and Blu – but Robert as well. Sure the guy was a total nuisance, but at least he was a consistent nuisance. For the past couple of years she'd come to know that she could always count on him to stick his nose in where it didn't belong or take some undeserved swipe at her for not wanting to go along with all his lame publicity schemes. Life would certainly be different without Robert around.

"Are you sleeping with your eyes open?" Robert snapped at her.

"What?"

Robert let out an annoyed sigh. "The photographer said he was done with this pose and asked you to go and sit on the nice horsie over there for your final pictures."

"Oh," Sam gritted her teeth sheepishly, "yeah. Okay. Sure thing."

Climbing up on the horse, Sam felt it nervously step back and forth.

"Whoa, big fella," she said as she patted the animal's neck. "I'm guessing this is about as much fun for you as it is for me. Don't worry. I won't hurt you."

Once everything was calm, the photographer began taking pictures and ordering Sam to look this way and that way, to smile bigger, but not that big. Sam tried to do exactly as the man was telling her – the sooner she could climb off the horse and scrub all the itchy makeup off her face the better.

"That's it, Miss," he finally said. "You can climb down."

Sam shifted her weight to swing her leg over the horse and hop down, but suddenly the quiet moment was interrupted by a harsh, loud car horn. This spooked the horse and he reared up, pawing the air with his front legs. Sam, being a natural horse rider, totally handled the moment. She threw herself forward and let herself gently fall back into the saddle as the horse came back down to the ground. Unfortunately, as she waited for the horse to settle, she heard a deafening scream that sounded a lot like Danni. Instinctively, Sam looked around to see if it indeed was her sister, but that movement caused her to lose her balance and tumble off the back of the horse. It all felt as if it were happening in slow motion, so as Sam was falling, she had the good sense to remind herself to roll away from the horse to avoid getting stepped on once she did hit the ground.

Olga and Carlos were the first people to reach her. Danni and Rose both raced out of the car they'd just pulled up in and the whole group stood over Sam.

"I'm fine!" Sam said as she waved her hands in the air. "No worries. I'm fine."

Danni dropped to her knees. "Sam!" she cried. "I'm so sorry! I'm such an idiot! I was so excited to tell you about the house I found that I honked and then screamed and almost got you killed!"

Robert put one arm around Danni. "She's fine. Look at her, no broken bones, no blood. Even I have to admit that seeing Sam roll off the horse like that was actually rather entertaining." He nodded down at Sam. "Where'd you learn to do that?"

She ignored him as she sat up. "Danni, it's no big deal."

With tears streaming down her cheeks, Danni clutched her heart. "I'm so sorry, Sam! I should have known better! Shouldn't we go to the hospital or something?"

Laughing as she took Carlos's hand to stand up, Sam shook her head. "Don't be crazy. I've taken much worse tumbles. This was nothing. Look," she pointed, "I didn't even hit the ground. I landed on some nice soft hay."

"Yes," Olga agreed, "some nice, soft, and seriously *stinky* hay."

"What?" Sam looked over at her friend and that's when the smell hit her. Ugh!

Rose put her fingers to her nose. "Oh, Samantha! You rolled right into horse dung. Oh that is *horrible*! You march right over to the stable's store and get yourself a new outfit."

"But, Mom," Sam whined, "it's just a little poop. I'll wrap myself in a blanket and clean up at home."

"Not a chance, Missy," her mother replied as she pointed over to the store. "I'm not having my daughter walking around in filthy clothes and you certainly aren't getting in the car in this state. Go get some new clothes and clean yourself up this minute. Robert will go with you to pay for whatever you want."

"I'll what?" he asked incredulously. "Rose, it's bad enough you sent me over here as a chaperone, now you're telling me to be the kid's personal shopper?"

Putting one arm around a still-shaking Danni, Rose gave him her famous, *do-not-question-my-authority* glare. "I'm not asking you to pick out the clothes, Robert, simply to pay for them. I need to help Danni calm down. Now both of you, go before that smell makes my nose melt like a popsicle in the July sun. Go!"

Olga joined Sam and Robert in the store.

"Picked something yet?" he barked at Sam's legs through the bottom of the dressing-room door.

Without giving Sam a moment to respond, he grabbed the closest pair of jeans and threw them over the door. "Here, take these."

From behind him, Olga's voice rang out with more than a hint of amusement in it. "Um, Mr. Ruebens, you're in the little kid section. Anything there will be way too small for Sam."

Holding up another pair of jeans to get a better look, Robert noticed the price tag. "You've got to be kidding. People pay this much for kiddie clothes?"

"Duh, Robert," Sam replied as she stepped out in a

clean T-shirt and plain jeans. "Why do you think I had to work here for so long before we had any money? Horse riding is expensive!"

Robert began walking around, checking out the prices for clothes, blankets, ropes, and other items on sale. "They charge this much for a shirt? And how much for that silly rope? People shell out this kind of dough to ride a smelly horse?"

Sam, Olga, and the lady behind the counter glared at Robert before turning their backs on him and completing the purchase of Sam's new outfit.

When the girls turned to hand Robert back his credit card, they were surprised to see that he'd already left. Sam grabbed the receipt and the girls headed back toward the main barn where they'd left Carlos, Rose, and Danni.

"Hey, Olga," Sam pointed as they walked, "why is Robert over there talking to your dad?"

She thought for a moment. "Maybe my dad is thanking him for helping out my mom with those fans earlier?"

"Maybe," Sam muttered, but in her head, she knew that Robert never wasted time being sociable.

Everything the guy did was somehow related to business; she wondered what new, annoying idea Robert could have that would involve Mr. Victorio.

CHAPTER 6

Click click click, clack clack click.

I've only got a couple of minutes to write because my sister just called a Devine family meeting. I'm hoping Danni has realized that moving out of the mansion and giving up singing is *wrong*. Hard to believe *I'm* saying this stuff, right? See, I did a lot of thinking yesterday.

It started when Robert told me he was worried about Danni and she needed a good vacation because she'd regret giving up her career and (big shocker alert) I AGREE WITH HIM (I had the idea first — but far be it from *Mr. White Teeth* to ever give ME any credit for anything). I can't stand the fact that I'm on the same side as him on anything — but this does make the most sense. Danni's worked beyond hard to become the major pop star she is today. For her to walk away from all that seems too sad, so I spent my whole evening searching for great places Danni could go and rest. There's three mind-blowing beach clubs in the Caribbean that look perfect. I'm bringing a stack of brochures I printed off. Here's my big plan:

#1 — Get Danni to *not* move out and *not* quit singing.

#2 — Help her pick the perfect vacation spot.

#3 — Get Robert to make sure the video crew DOES NOT follow us so Danni can get some serious relaxation.

#4 – Go on the trip with Danni to make sure all she does is chill and have fun.

#5 – Come back home with a happy sister and a relaxed mom so we can return to our "normal" life (HA! To think that living my life on TV is normal).

That sounds totally logical, don't you think? Whoops – just got yelled at to get down to the meeting! Wish me luck!

Armed with her stack of brochures, Sam grabbed her usual seat at the dining room table. Normally, a family meeting took place with a big spread of food, but at this one there was nothing – not even a bottle of water.

Michi and Lou were both fidgeting with their equipment. Sam smiled at them and then giggled thinking how annoyed Robert would be to see her acknowledging their existence. As Sam waited for the meeting to begin, she noticed that Rose, sitting in her normal seat on the other side of the table, had a worried expression on her face.

"Don't worry, Mom," she whispered, "I've got a plan that's a big win-win for everybody."

Rose nodded, but she didn't really seem to have heard Sam. Robert, however, standing behind his chair at the head of the table, rolled his eyes.

Sam saw this and very matter-of-factly said, "You wait and see."

Danni walked into the dining room with her own stack of papers. Instead of taking her traditional seat in the middle of the table, she went straight up to the front and waited for Robert to move. There was a weird silent power struggle as Robert stared at Danni staring back at him, but without any fighting or drama, he picked up his coffee cup and moved over to Danni's normal chair on the other side of Rose.

Oh boy, Sam thought, *this is so not going to be a normal family meeting*. But she had her plan and her determination to fix everything didn't waver a bit.

"Thank you for joining me this morning," Danni spoke in her *I'm all business* voice.

"Thank *you* for being willing to talk about stuff," Sam echoed her sister's serious tone. She wanted to appear all positive to make sure Danni would be open to her vacation ideas. "It's wonderful to have a chance to chat calmly about everything that's happened over the past couple of days."

No one spoke, but Robert did move his hand over his mouth to cover up what looked to Sam suspiciously like a grin. She wanted to snap at him not to laugh at her – she was conducting big-time business here – but she maintained her focus and continued talking.

"Danni, I know you've had a lot going on and I *so* seriously support you in everything—" Sam began to push the brochures toward her sister, but Danni interrupted her.

"I'm glad to hear that, Little Bit," she said forcefully, "because I called my lawyer this morning and told her to do whatever it took to buy me the house I saw yesterday."

"Dannielle Ann Devine!" Rose slapped her hand on the table. "You cannot make such a big decision by yourself! I know you liked that place, but buying a home is a very serious decision. An eighteen-year-old doesn't do something like this without at least one very serious discussion with her mother."

"Sorry, Mom," Danni answered, "but I can and I did. I just got a text saying that my offer was accepted and I should be able to move into my new home in thirty days' time." She turned to Sam. "You'll love the place, Little Bit. It's got a whole room with these huge built-in shelves. We'll go to the bookstore and you can buy all the books you want!"

"But, but Danni," Sam stammered as her eyes began to fill with tears, "I don't need anymore books. I…I don't want you to leave. Here," she pushed the brochures down the table, "wouldn't you rather spend a couple of weeks on a beach with me than be all alone in some empty old house?"

Danni smiled at her little sister. "That's super-sweet, Sam, but I need to do this. Listen, this house has *three* bedrooms. I'm hoping you'll come and stay whenever you want so I won't be *so* alone, but I do need to live on my own. It's time. I know in my heart this is the right thing to do."

"Do you understand the enormity of this decision?" Robert asked quietly. "You aren't just ending your performing career." He leaned over the table. "Your decision affects a whole host of people." He waved his hand toward Michi and Lou. "The TV crew, your hair and makeup artists, if you quit everything, this entire group of professionals will be out of a job. Now, if you agreed to stay here in the house, not to move out, we *might* be able to work out some deal with the production company to keep the show alive for one more season."

Sighing, Danni nodded. "Of course I feel terrible about putting everyone out of work, but you said it yourself – these people *are* professionals. Every single one of them will be able to find another gig. I can't live my life being stressed and unhappy just to keep other people employed."

"What about my employment?" Robert pointed at his chest. "You brushed me off when I mentioned it before, but this is serious. You have a legal contract with me. The only reason you have all the money to buy that fancy new house is because of the time and effort I put in to building your career. You expect me simply to wave as you skip away, taking a good portion of my income with you?"

Danni looked momentarily stunned, but she pulled herself together. "I know I owe you huge, Robert, I owe you everything! But you don't want a client who's miserable. If you feel you have to sue me, then go ahead. You know as well as I do that it'll end up bringing you a lot more bad publicity than it will me."

"But where will we go?" Sam looked over at Rose. "This means we have to move too, right, Mom? We can't stay here if we aren't doing the TV show anymore, right? Am I right?"

Rose held up her hands as if to calm Sam. "Let me worry about that, Sweetie." She spoke softly. "Your old mom still has a few tricks up her sleeve."

The ringing of the doorbell broke the silence that had fallen over the room. Danni ran to get it and returned a moment later with a young man carrying a large binder.

"This is Thomas, everyone. He's a fabulous decorator. He and I are going up to my room to discuss the amazing ideas he has for my new home."

"Excuse me, young lady," Rose stood up from her chair, "this meeting is not over yet. Your gentleman caller can wait, and when we *are* done, I would prefer if you two would work in the living room rather than in your bedroom."

"Oh, Mother," Danni laughed. "Don't be so old-fashioned."

"Good manners and a little decorum are *not* old-fashioned," Rose replied coldly.

"Relax, Mom." Danni waved her hand as if she was dismissing a mosquito. "Sam," she said as she walked out with Thomas following close behind, "*you* are welcome to come up and see all our fabulous design ideas."

With Danni gone, the meeting came to a screeching end. Rose sat back down. She raised her hands and rubbed her temples.

"It's okay, Mom," Sam said even though she wasn't really sure it was.

"I'll call the producers right away." Robert reached for his Blackberry. "I'm sure there's some deal we can cut for you and Sam to stay in this house."

"No, Robert." Rose reached out and put her hand on his to stop him. "Don't do anything yet." She took a moment before looking over at him. "Am I wrong? Am I too old-fashioned? Danni is eighteen. At her age, most young women are moving out to go to college. But to have gone out and bought her own house?

This is her house. *This* is our family *home*. It doesn't seem right to me."

Robert shook his head. "I'm out of my league here, Rose," he said kindly. "Family dynamics are beyond my expertise. All I can tell you is that I think you've done a first-class job raising Danni."

Raising Danni? What was Sam then – an afterthought? Without realizing it, Sam let out an aggravated snort that actually startled both Robert and Rose.

With dry humor in his voice, Robert nodded over toward Sam, "And yes, even *that one* hasn't turned out *too* badly."

Rose giggled softly. Sam was relieved to see the tension lighten. She was going to run to her mom and give her a hug, but as she stood, she noticed Robert putting his hand on Rose's shoulder. Rose, in turn, patted Robert's hand.

It felt to Sam as if she was witnessing something she wasn't supposed to. Mom and Robert getting all cozy – yech! She couldn't watch another moment. Silently she slipped away and back up to her bedroom. Plopping herself onto her bed, she pulled her cell phone out of her pocket and dialed Olga.

It took two rings for Olga to answer and two minutes for Sam to recount the drama of the family meeting.

"Don't move," her best friend ordered. "I'm already walking over to the garage to get my bike. I'll be there ASAP. Hey, should I bring Carlos or would that make things even more complicated for you?"

"You can invite him," Sam replied. "He was so awesome yesterday at the stables. I never got to thank him for helping to lift me out of the horse poop."

"He must really like you," Olga answered back. "Remember, he's a city boy. He isn't into horses or farm stuff. For him to be willing to hang at the stables for the day and then lend a hand to a girl covered in stinky horse apples, I think it says something."

Sam snorted, "Hardly. He was probably hoping I'd broken a bone or fractured something so he could get a head start on his medical studies."

That made Olga giggle. "See you in a few."

When Olga and Carlos arrived, the three of them headed out into the backyard. As they sat down next to the pool, Olga opened the bag she had brought with her and pulled out three cans of orange cream soda.

"I figured if ever your mom was going to let you have a treat, it would be today," she said as she handed Sam a can.

"Thanks mucho," Sam replied before slugging down a huge gulp.

Carlos took a sip and made a sour face. "This is awful!" he exclaimed.

That made both girls laugh. Everyone kicked off their shoes and dunked their feet in the pool.

"Carlos knows about your family meeting," Olga told Sam.

"Pretty messed up, don't you think?" Sam shook her head. "And that part at the end, where my mom looked so sad? I think that's the worst of it all. It was nice of Robert to at least try and help her."

"I don't understand." Carlos sat up a little straighter. "From what Olga has told me, I thought he was a bad guy, but it sounds like he's done some nice things for your family."

Sam nodded begrudgingly. "Yeah, I know. He has become Mom's go-to guy for all kinds of stuff. I still can't believe he took me to the stables this morning and came shopping for my new clothes." She giggled.

"Although considering how bad I stunk, he may have done that just to save his own sense of smell." She sighed. "Maybe he figured after all the trouble he'd caused, the least he could do was make my mom's life a little easier as things gets weirder."

Olga took another drink before asking, "Sam, does your mom ever talk about your dad?"

"Not in front of me." Sam slapped her feet against the top of the water. "When money was really tight, I would sometimes hear her talking to his picture, asking him to help her make good decisions and find a job that would support us. One time I heard her crying to him because she was afraid we wouldn't have enough money for that month's rent." She paused for a second as the sadness of the memory filled her head. "I haven't heard any of that since Danni began working with Robert and all the money started coming in, but now with Danni quitting..." Sam's voice trailed off.

"I get it," Carlos agreed. "Having to worry about money again will be a big stress for an old person."

Sam laughed. "My mom's not old." But then she stopped and thought. Rose was mega-energetic and didn't dress or act like an old lady, but she wasn't a kid either. "But she is a *lot* older than she was when Dad died and she first had to take over all the family finances. Maybe you have a point. Since he died her entire life has been about taking care of Danni and me. I remember when she had to do two jobs to keep us afloat. Having plenty of money and not freaking out over finding work the past two years has *finally* given her the chance to have some fun in her life. Mind you, *her* idea of *fun* – shopping or attending fancy parties and having it all videotaped to share with Planet Earth – that's been total torture for me."

Carlos looked at her. "Has being on TV been that awful? It seems like it would be an interesting thing to do."

Sam grimaced. "Interesting? Okay, sure, it's been *interesting* – but that doesn't even begin to describe the humiliation of having every stupid little thing you do or say watched by a gazillion people. You can't imagine how terrible it is to try and do something as simple as going to a restaurant. One time, we were waiting for a table, and I, totally innocently, asked this lady what was the," Sam raised her hands to make air quotes, "wait – w-a-i-t – *wait*. But she thought I meant *weight*,"

Sam opened her arms out wide, "w-e-i-g-h-t – *weight,* and the lady got all insulted. She yelled at me, at Danni, and made a nightmare of a scene. Then that ended up on our TV show and I got tons of mail from people who thought I was rude, insensitive, and mean to fat people. It was horrible! Even now, I'm still dealing with the baloney of the great *Sam Gets a Zit* episode and when that goes into repeats, I'll be hearing about it for the rest of my life!" She suddenly got massively embarrassed, realizing she'd admitted to a boy she liked – the one person who it seemed hadn't been following her life on TV for the past two years – that she had indeed had a pimple. Red-faced, she turned to Olga. "You understand, don't you? Isn't it awful for you when people know all kinds of private stuff about your family because they are famous?"

Olga flinched. "Yeah, I still see pics on the internet of my mom falling on the runway and her panties hanging out for the whole world to see. It kills me. But your mom does seem to enjoy it and she sure loves this house. Maybe you need to figure out a way to keep the show going without Danni. Wait!" Olga snapped her finger. "What if *you* become the focus of

The Devine Life so it could stay on the air?"

"Me?" Sam's feet shot out of the pool so fast that water flew all over Olga and Carlos. "You're so joking, right?"

"Hear me out." Olga wiped the water from her eyes. "You have to do the reality show for *three* years to own the house, right?"

Sam nodded.

"And you've survived *two* so far, right?" Olga asked.

Sam rolled her eyes, but nodded again.

Olga clapped her hands. "All you need is one more year and everything is good! We need to figure out an angle to keep the show focused on you rather than Danni, and in twelve months, you walk away with a family home and more money in the bank!"

"You make it sound so easy." Sam gripped the side of the pool. Being a *part* of a reality show was bad enough, but thinking about becoming the sole focus of those annoying cameras and microphones made her dizzy. "I'm not interesting enough for people to watch week after week. At least now, as bad as it is, I'm usually just a sidebar story to whatever is going on in Danni's world."

"But you could change all that." Olga pointed at Sam. "True, you're no pop star, but there's no reason why you couldn't do something equally interesting that'd be worth recording. Think about it! If you can keep the reality show alive for just *one more year,* your mom would *never* have to worry about paying the rent again!"

Carlos kicked water at his cousin. "Maybe she could star in one of your father's silly telenovella stories."

"Hush up, you," Olga snipped at Carlos. "Seriously, Sam, there's got to be *something* you could do to hold onto the reality show for just one more year."

Sam put a hand on her stomach to try and help it settle down. "This conversation is making me sick. I can't imagine life getting anymore complicated."

"Good point." Olga nodded. "We need to find something that won't add any complications. You've already accepted the fact that you need to be stuck in reality TV for one more year, so what if we could make it something you could kind of enjoy? Hold up, I've got it!" Olga pointed over toward the stables. "*Horses!* You're an excellent rider! You know more about taking care of horses than most vets. You could refocus the show on that! Every episode of *The Devine Life* could be about you visiting different stables and learning from other great riders. I'd watch that! Carlos and I could help you map it all out so you could present it to Robert. Let's each think about it overnight and meet tomorrow to…oh wait…we have to register Carlos for school tomorrow." Olga thought for a moment. "No worries, the day after tomorrow will work. We'll meet here right after lunch the day after tomorrow. That'll give us a little more time to get our ideas down on paper."

"Be careful, Sam," Carlos warned. "Olga is a hopeless dreamer. Do you know she stays up late to watch all those silly adventures and cheesy love stories on that awful Romance channel?"

"Zip it, *chistoso*." Olga glared at Carlos. "Those movies aren't silly; they show strong women standing up for themselves when everything around them has fallen apart. They are very inspirational!" She turned back to Sam with an excited smile. "Think about it! It *would* be just like one of those movies: the little sister comes out from behind the shadow of her big sis to do something heroic and saves her family from total ruin!

It would make a great book; you could write it later and make even more money to take care of your mom! For once, you'd be the brave, beautiful heroine of the story instead of the wacky, comic relief!"

Being called *beautiful* embarrassed Sam, but she was still stuck on the idea of being able to take care of her mom. "I suppose I *could* talk to Robert about trying to keep *The Devine Life* alive for just one more season with me teaching horse care and giving great riding tips...and I could add in telling people about awesome charities, like the *STARS* program. That would be rockin' cool. It couldn't hurt to at least ask, right?"

"Right!" Olga threw her hands in the air with so much emphatic energy that she threw herself forward and teetered precariously on the edge of the pool. Sam reached out to steady her, but in the process of trying to help, lost her balance and tumbled into the pool.

CHAPTER 7

Sam sat in front of her computer blankly. She wanted to blog about her conversation with Olga and Carlos, but no words seemed to make enough sense to type out. The far-off sound of someone knocking on her door snuck into her very busy brain.

"Come in," she mumbled, while staring out of her window. Her thoughts were zooming all over the place. Talk to Robert about becoming the sole focus of *The Devine Life*? Olga had convinced her it was a great idea, but now, alone in her room, it sounded even crazier than when she'd first heard it. Could she do anything, even with horses, that would make people want to watch? How could she take on the responsibility of earning money to help her mom when she could barely handle something as basic as her crush on Carlos? Carlos! He'd jumped into the pool after her when she'd fallen in. It was really mortifying, especially since she'd fallen into the shallow end and the only thing that got hurt was the cell phone in her pocket – which was now on her window sill drying out, *hopefully*! How cool was it of Carlos to try and save her? But then again, the guy wants to be a doctor some day; he was probably excited over the thought of getting to save somebody – not Sam in particular. Or, maybe he'd jumped in so fast to help his *friend*, Sam – not the Sam he *liked* liked.

The knocking behind her happened again, but was much louder.

"I said *come in*," she shouted.

"I heard you the first time," Robert's annoyed voice shot back, "but when you didn't respond to my 'do you have a moment' question, I thought I'd start over."

"Oh, uh…sorry." Sam was embarrassed to have been caught so lost in her own thoughts. "Okay." Then it hit her, what was Robert doing coming up to speak to her? "What do you...um...hi?"

Leaning against the door, Robert seemed amused by Sam's confusion. "I have a meeting tomorrow morning and I thought you might enjoy coming along."

"Me?" Sam was stunned. She folded her arms in front of her. "Why?"

"Because my meeting is with someone I think you'd enjoy getting to know."

Sam bit her lip. If she was going through with her plan to take care of Rose and keep the house, then she needed to get it through Robert's thick skull that he had to stop talking to her in his snotty, businesslike, *you can't handle the truth* way that always drove her up the wall!

Sitting up straight, she answered, "Robert, I would seriously appreciate it if you could, from now on, give me the whole story when you speak to me. *Who* is the meeting with and *why* would I enjoy getting to know this person?"

Robert nodded. "All right. I can appreciate that. However, I've been doing business this way for twenty years and even *you* have to admit I've been rather successful. Yes?"

Hold the phone! Robert was speaking to her like she was a…a…a real human – not an annoying little kid! This was majorly new territory.

"Yes," she said plainly.

"Okay then." Robert pushed away from the door. "I'll be here at nine a.m. Please be ready."

As he walked out of her room, Sam thought to call him back to discuss her idea for saving the show, but instead of keeping her mind on the plan, she found herself wondering what was going on; Robert had said *please* to her. He had actually been kind of polite. *What's up with that?* she wondered. *Is he trying to do something to please my mom because he's worried about her too?*

That night, Sam felt so much confusion over everything that she stayed in her room watching more of those old Muppet videos online. The lack of drama and the simple pleasures of the gags and silly songs helped her chill out.

The next day, Robert drove up at exactly nine o' clock. The car ride to the meeting was weird – not bad – just weird. Sam wanted to begin her negotiations for saving *The Devine Life*, but she lost her focus with the fun exhilaration of traveling in a sports car. It was sleek and went super-fast. The only bummer moment was when Robert made her tie back her hair because it was whipping around in the wind so much, it kept hitting him in the eyes, making driving dangerous.

The car pulled up in front of a wicked cool beach club. The long building stretched out for almost a mile. Looking through the giant windows, you could see the ocean and the beautiful white sand. Sam was so thrilled at the sight that she forgot about the meeting and got busy wondering how mad her mom would be if she came home with her clothes all wet from splashing around in the water.

"Come on," Robert said as he stood on the front steps, "it's much easier to be *in* the meeting if you get *out* of the car and *enter* the building."

Sam hopped out and followed him in. As they entered the dining room, she was very surprised to see Michi and Lou already videotaping them from a corner of the room.

"We drove all the way here for Michi and Lou?" she asked.

"Not quite," Robert answered as he scanned the room.

"Robert Ruebens!" a voice called out behind them.

Sam turned to see a teenage boy wearing a baseball cap, who was maybe a year or two older than her, walking toward them with a huge, handsome grin on his face. *Whoa*, she thought, *he's beautiful!* The thought embarrassed her enough to turn her cheeks bright red.

Robert shook hands with the teenager and then stepped back. "Sam Devine, meet Seth Black. I'm sure you recognize Seth from all his TV and movie work. He's been acting since he was five—"

"Four," Seth interrupted. "I shot my first commercial when I was four."

"Sorry," Robert smiled at Seth, but then returned his attention to Sam, "since he was four. This young man here is a total pro. I wanted you two to get to know each other and see how well you get along."

Sam could only nod. Was this a set-up? Had Robert dragged her all the way to the beach for some kind of first date? No matter, *holy guacamole* was this guy good-looking!

The three sat at their table and looked over the breakfast menu. Every now and then Sam peered over at Michi and Lou. Why were they here? Was this just another embarrassing moment for the TV show?

The waiter took everyone's order. Sam, so self-conscious she could barely speak, had simply said, "Me too," after Seth ordered steak and eggs, even though it sounded like way too much food.

Seth seemed really nice. He asked Sam all kinds of questions about what books she liked and how much she enjoyed her time riding and working at the SuAn Stables. He appeared to know an awful lot about her for somebody she'd never met before.

Robert's Blackberry rang. He excused himself to take the call out in the lobby. Sam watched him get up and leave the room, but inside she was screaming for him to sit back down and not leave her alone with Seth!

Once it was just the two of them, Seth leaned in toward Sam and asked in a hushed voice, "So, you think this will work?"

Completely freaked out and not having a clue what he was referring to, Sam whispered back, "Work?"

Seth smiled and pointed back and forth between the two of them. "You and me, as a team, starring in our own TV show. Didn't Robert tell you?" He studied

Sam's face and started to laugh. "I guess he didn't. Yeah, I can understand. He wanted to be sure you and I got along before he gave you the great news."

Both Sam and Seth leaned back as the waiter brought over their drinks and set them on the table. Seth took a sip of his before yelling out, "Yo, dude! Are you sure this is a sugar-free soda? It tastes too good to be sugar free."

The waiter assured Seth that indeed it was, but Seth was insistent. "Listen, I know what sugar free tastes like and this isn't sugar free. Take it back and bring me a real sugar-free soda."

Yikes! Sam had never seen somebody her own age speak so rudely to an adult. If she'd ever done something like that, her mom would have boxed her ears, made her apologize that minute, and grounded her for a month. Not only that, but why was Seth wearing his baseball cap *inside* the restaurant? Even Sam knew that was bad manners.

Seth quickly turned his attention back to Sam and returned to being the charming guy he'd been a minute before. "Here's the scoop. My agent called me the other night and explained that your agent, Robert, was putting together a new family TV show. It would star you and me. You'd be the sweet, funny, poor girl who works at the horse stables and I'd be the cool, rich boy whose family expects him to win an Olympic gold medal in riding before taking over the family business, but then you fall in love with me and it messes with all their plans. Apparently there's already a hot director attached to the project. So, you in? Robert told me how much you love horses and you seem pretty cool; it's awesome that you're new to acting. You won't have any bad habits or try to upstage me. I'm great to work with. I always know my lines and am ready and willing to do whatever publicity is necessary to make the project a success."

Sam leaned forward to take a sip of her soda, not because she was thirsty, but to buy her some time to think before speaking. Her thoughts were a total mess. A TV show? A new TV show? She'd be *starring* in a real TV show? With Seth Black – someone she obviously should have recognized but didn't. She glanced up at the camera crew, desperately wanting to grab the earpiece from Michi and talk to Blu, but in doing so, she leaned her face in the wrong direction and instead of getting a sip of soda, she got the straw up her nose.

Seth stared at Sam as if she were completely insane before totally cracking up. "That's great! I love it," he chortled. "Physical humor – it isn't my thing, but it plays brilliantly on TV. This show is going to be a huge hit! Come on, Sam, you and me riding horses and having a ball shooting a TV show. How buzzing would that be? I'm in! Say you're in, too!"

Sam tried to play along while trying to figure out if *buzzing* was good or bad. "Um...I guess...I'm in."

Seth stood up as Robert returned to the table. "Thanks for setting up this meet and greet, Robert. It went very well. Sorry, but I've got to dash; got a video chat with a director for a Japanese car commercial. I'm a *mega*-celebrity over there, so how could I not do something that would let my fans see me more often?" He gave Sam a heart-melting grin. "It was solid getting to know you, Sam. I'm stoked you're a yes on the show! Oh, hey – I almost forgot. My agent had a great idea; how about you joining me for my favorite yoga class tomorrow afternoon? The teacher is the hottest thing in town, everyone is fighting to get in, but she *loves* me.

She'll be cool with me bringing a guest. So, you in? You do *do* yoga, right?"

Robert gave Seth a friendly pat on the back. "Of course she does. How do you think our girl stays in such great shape? You reserve the space and I'll be sure to get her to class on time. Have your assistant e-mail my assistant the info. Thanks again for coming, Seth. Talk to you soon."

Robert sat down and motioned for the waiter to come over. He said something about canceling Seth's order, but Sam wasn't listening. She couldn't believe what had just happened. She leaned forward and, managing this time to get the straw into her mouth, sipped down her entire soda. When she sat back up, Robert was staring at her.

"Seth told you about the show?"

Sam nodded.

"And right now you're a little overwhelmed?"

Sam nodded again.

Robert carefully placed both his hands on the table. "That's fair. Let me explain. This will be a family show set at the stables, something you'll enjoy doing and watching with your mom."

"Does my mom know about this?"

"Yes. Of course. Well, kind of." Robert looked a little uncomfortable for the first time. Sam knew that look, it meant he was searching for the right way to say something rather than just giving her the whole truth. "I mentioned it to her but she didn't think you'd be interested."

That was all Sam needed to hear. She stood up and prepared to walk out, but Robert kept talking.

"However, I told her that I believed you'd have a wonderful time shooting the show and would want to do it. Besides, with Danni not working, how do you think your mom is going to manage financially?"

That caught Sam's attention. So maybe Robert wasn't just being greedy and selfish; maybe he was thinking about what was best for Rose and wanted to be sure that she had enough money. Sam sat back down.

"Keep talking," she said.

"Money goes quickly when there isn't anymore coming in, trust me on this. With Danni not performing or cutting any new records, your mom will need to figure out how to bring in more cash fast. Once Rose officially becomes your manager, she'll continue having an income, plus, by doing *this* show, *The Devine Life* stays on the air and you can stay in the mansion," he continued, speaking very quickly. "Mr. Victorio and I had a brainstorm at the stables the other night. There is a huge worldwide market for anything related to horse riding. A family TV show is cheap to produce and the opportunities for product placement are mind-numbingly obvious. While you aren't a real actress, you are a celebrity and people already associate you with horses – so it's an easy fit. Mr. Victorio will produce the show, so that gives us immediate cred with selling the show in foreign markets. It'll air on the T2CT channel on Saturdays, when younger people watch. We can shoot it at the SuAn Stables to keep the costs down and you won't have to move or drive far away to go to work. Think about it, Samantha. It's a one-year contract and at the end of it, you'll get to keep the mansion, free and clear! You—"

"Wait." Sam shook her head. "You want me to take over my sister's reality show *and* star in my own family show?"

"Exactly!" Robert pounded the table enthusiastically.

Before Sam could ask exactly what it all meant, Robert launched into the rest of his big sales push. "You and your mom won't have to worry one bit about money or a place to live. Plus, not that this will mean very much to you, we will keep the entire production staff from the reality show so Michi and Lou and Jean and Jehan – everyone who is currently working on *The Devine Life* will still have jobs and be around. You do like all those people, right?"

Sam's heart began to race. Had her major earth-shaking, heartbreaking problems just been completely fixed? If Robert had arranged for the reality show to stay on the air and they kept *everyone* from *The Devine Life* that meant she got to take care of her mom and keep Blu in her life! Still, one thing was buzzing around in her and she just had to ask.

"Umm…" she tried to appear very casual, "Seth said something about a hot director for our show. Who do you have in mind?"

Robert waved his hand. "It's nobody you know. We'll use the same guy who has been directing your sister's show. His name is Malcolm Bluford. He's a rock solid professional. You'll enjoy working with him."

That sealed the deal. Sam reached out her hand toward Robert. "Okay, Mr. Agent," she said, trying to contain her bubbling enthusiasm, "I'm in."

Robert wanted to leave that minute to begin working, but the waiter brought their breakfast and Sam was really hungry. As she dug in to her ridiculously huge meal, she tried to get a grip on everything that had just happened. By agreeing to be in this new TV show, she'd ensured that her mom would have plenty of money, she'd saved Michi, Lou, Jean, Jehan and Blu from the unemployment line, she'd managed to buy herself a whole ton of time at the stables, and now she could be friends with Blu *for reals* and talk to him any time she liked! The only thing that was bothering her was Seth. He was beyond good-looking, but there was something about him that rubbed her the wrong way. Why had he been so rude to the waiter? Who would wear a *baseball cap* in a classy restaurant? What was that whole thing about getting her into the *big deal* yoga class? Oh! Yoga class! He'd said that was tomorrow afternoon, but Sam had already made plans to hang with Olga and Carlos tomorrow afternoon.

"Robert," she said with a mouthful of eggs, "I can't go to yoga tomorrow with Seth. If you forward me his e-mail, I'll tell him myself."

"'Fraid not, kiddo," Robert replied. "We need that boy. He's a much bigger name than you." He paused to choke down a little laugh. "Although the kid is not as big a star as he likes to think. Still, he will get top billing and if we lose him, we lose the show. You'll go to yoga and anywhere else he invites you. Think of it as pre-show publicity. People seeing the two of you out and about will get a good buzz going."

"But I've never done yoga. I don't know a thing about it. I'll look like a total doofus."

"All the better." Robert smiled his frighteningly white grin. "You are the show's comic relief. Anything funny you do in real life will simply add to your reputation as a comedian."

Sam slumped down into her chair. One minute she was little Miss Nobody and now suddenly she had a reputation as a comedian to worry about.

"One last thing," Robert managed to speak while simultaneously eating his salad and typing on his Blackberry, "let *me* explain all this to your mom."

Sighing with relief at the thought of avoiding that conversation, Sam happily nodded and shoved another forkful of eggs into her mouth.

There wasn't much else to say. Once they'd finished eating, Robert drove Sam home. She went straight up to her room, sat on her bed, and stared at her feet. She needed to push her plans with Olga and Carlos. The fact that her cell phone was on the fritz from its dip in the pool yesterday was a totally lame excuse for not contacting them that minute, but seeing as she so badly didn't want to explain to her friends *why* she had to bail on them, she just sat there, doing nothing but feeling unexpectedly icky inside.

That night, dinner in the Devine house began on a really weird note. It was as if everyone was afraid to speak; even Michi and Lou, videotaping the meal, seemed on edge. Rose had ordered in some delicious Indian food, but no one was in a rush to put anything on their plates. It felt to Sam as if everybody was waiting for someone else to speak first.

"So, Danni," she chirped in a forced, light tone, "anything new in your house-buying major redecorating world?"

"Everything is going super-great, thanks," Danni replied as she reached for a serving spoon and began heaping curry and rice onto her plate. "In fact, I have an announcement: we've been able to complete all the paperwork faster than expected and I get to take possession of the house exactly *two weeks from today*!"

Rose looked stunned. "That fast? But before you said something about thirty days! How can the sale of something as big as a house go through this quickly? Are you sure it's all above board?"

"Don't worry, Rose," Robert said as he handed her a plate of food. "I've been in touch with Danni's lawyer and everything is fine. In fact, since she's paying cash for the house, she got a great deal. You should be proud of your daughter for handling this transaction so well. She's learned a great deal about business from you and it's paying off."

"Thank you, Robert." Danni seemed genuinely touched by his words. "I was thinking that on that date, before I move, as a big finale for the reality show—"

"About that," Robert raised his hand, "sorry to interrupt you, Danni, but I too have an announcement.

The Devine Life reality show is not ending; it's going to continue for another season with the focus shifting from Danni as a pop star to Sam as a budding TV actress."

Sam lowered her head, but glanced around to see her mom and Danni's reactions. Rose appeared pleased, but Danni's face scrunched up into a grimace.

"Are you talking about that *Stables Stories* idea I heard you pitching to Mr. Victorio the other day?" she asked.

Robert nodded.

Danni looked back and forth between Robert and Rose before getting up from her seat and going over to sit next to Sam.

"Listen up, Little Bit," she said gently. "This is serious stuff. Being a working performer means giving away a huge chunk of your life. You are always on show; people are watching and discussing and judging your every move. You've only had a small taste of it so far being a part of our reality show. If you go through with this sitcom thing it's opening the door to a major new level of responsibility, drama, and intrusion. You'll be working morning, noon, and night. Even when you go to a party, you won't be able to have fun because you'll have to *work the room*. You'll need to be seen and photographed talking to the *right people* all the time. You won't have any time for your friends and pretty soon you won't be able to tell your real friends from the people clinging on to you because they want something from you – as if your being famous will somehow rub off on them and make their lives better. I don't want you to end up as exhausted and fed up as I am right now. Are you *sure* you want to do this?"

Forcing a bright, happy grin on her face, Sam playfully slapped her hands on the table. "Of course I want to do it! What could be better than getting paid to spend all day at the stables? I'm excited about it… very, very excited!"

"All right." Danni still wasn't convinced. "But what about continuing the reality show? Out of the three of us – you, Mom and me – you've always been the first one to complain. How many times have you ditched poor Michi and Lou when they were just doing their jobs filming you? That's not going to fly if you're the center of the whole show. Are you sure you're ready for your whole life to be on TV?"

Sam couldn't look her sister in the eye; instead she stared directly into the camera lens. "I am. I am ready for my life to be on TV. In fact, we could even change the name of the show to *My Life on TV* – that's how ready I am."

Robert laughed and patted Sam on the shoulder. "See, Rose. I told you she wanted this. You have nothing to worry about."

Rose shrugged wearily. "Okay then. It appears the decision has been made, but Samantha," her voice became soft and serious, "if you find that this is all too much for you, I need you to tell me. I'm still your mother – and TV star or not – you are still my little girl and I care more about your happiness than anything else. Understand?"

Sam nodded. Even though part of her wanted to admit that she was freaked out by all these changes, her need to take care of her mom and keep Blu in her life was more important, so she pushed her doubts aside and picked up her fork. "All righty then, let's dig in. I'm starving."

"One more thing," Danni called out, "I hadn't finished *my* announcement before I was interrupted by

Robert with *his* announcement. Seeing as I am retiring, I want to end my career on a positive note. I want to do one last concert, not a huge one, but something small and very special; I want it to be a benefit for the *STARS* program to try and make it up to Rowan and all those kids I disappointed before. What do you think?"

Sam ran around the table and gave her sister a big hug. "I think that's the best idea you've ever had."

Rose's eyes welled up. "Sweetie, that is a classy thing to do."

"You know," Robert chimed in, "we could hold your farewell concert at the SuAn Stables and schedule it for the evening after Sam's first day of shooting. We'll have plenty of lights and equipment already there. That's two weeks away. We'll have time to publicize the event and it'll be great PR for Sam's new show."

"That's brilliant," Rose said. "I love it."

"Then I'll get right on it," Robert said as he reached for his Blackberry.

"Robert," Rose asked quietly, "could you please refrain from using that thing during dinner? The four of us won't have many more meals together. Would you try to remain present rather than spending the whole time chattering away with someone else?"

Sam expected Robert to launch into one of his famous, *but I'm a very busy man* speeches, but he didn't. He set down the phone and picked up his fork.

The table went silent again. Sam had never had Indian food before and while the curry was pretty tasty, the lamb kebabs weren't tickling her taste buds. She tried to chew and swallow, all the while worrying about how she was going to explain to Olga and Carlos about having to cancel their plans tomorrow. Finally, realizing that the lamb just wasn't working for her she absent-mindedly asked, "Could somebody please pass the Carlos?"

Everyone at the table stared at her. It took a moment before she realized what had come out of her mouth.

"Ketchup!" she yelled. "I mean ketchup! Could somebody please—"

Sam stopped speaking because it was useless. Rose, Robert, Danni, Michi, and Lou were all too busy laughing to hear anything else she said. With her cheeks burning hot from embarrassment, Sam slipped out of her chair and bolted up to her room.

Click click click, clack clack click.

I can't tell you how I'm feeling right now because there is no one word in the whole English language to describe it; if you could add humiliation and mortification and multiply them by infinity – then you'd be *close*. (sigh)

I accidentally said something at dinner that made my whole family laugh at me. I'm in my room now and my mom has buzzed me four times on the intercom to come back down to dinner, but I just can't. Me and my stupid mouth!

Everything is changing so fast. It's like I was riding a nice merry-go-round that suddenly turned into a rocket. Somehow I agreed to be in a new TV show – that *sounds* great, don't you think? But now I'm having serious second thoughts. Being famous has totally stressed out my sister. Am I a doofus for going down the same path? I've got a huge list of reasons why doing the show is a good idea, so why am I being such a major chicken about calling my best friend to discuss it with her? If I have to postpone or cancel plans with Olga and Carlos because of work, they'll understand, won't they? But is going to yoga class with my TV co-star really work? URGH! Life shouldn't be this confusing; I thought agreeing to be in this new TV show would make everything all right. Forget that.

In fact, right now, I need to forget all about all this. I'm going to pretend none of it is happening. As far as I'm concerned, it's summer again, I'm bored to death, and I'm going to watch some Muppet videos and go to bed.

CHAPTER 8

"Rise and shine, Sweetie!"

Sam awoke to see her mom drawing back the curtains in her bedroom. She'd hardly slept the night before, so she wasn't in the mood for a super-cheery wake-up call. She pulled the covers over her head and hoped her mom would go away.

"Come on, Sam," Rose twittered. "You've got a big day ahead of you. I understand you've got a date this afternoon."

That made her sit up. "Mom," she whined. "It's not a date!"

"All right," giggled Rose, "it's not a date. It's an

appointment. It's pre-show publicity. Either way, Robert and I discussed everything and if you're going to do this TV show, you're going to do it right. Get out of bed, get dressed, come down for breakfast, and let's figure out what you're going to wear to this non-date appointment thing."

After her mom left, Sam slowly moved from her bed over to her computer chair. She clicked the button to check her e-mail and saw something from Olga.

Carlos and I have some amazing ideas for reinventing The Devine Life, it read.

Meet at your place around 2:00? Lady O

Sam bit her lip. She'd never ever lied to Olga, but to come out and say she didn't need any help saving the reality show and that she was bailing on her friends for a yoga class with Seth Black (whom she'd Googled the previous night and discovered truly was a kind of famous guy) didn't seem right. But this was a business thing! Robert had made it clear that they needed Seth for the show and Sam was supposed to do whatever she could to keep him happy, and it seemed that going out in public together, an obvious publicity stunt, was what made Seth happy. Thus, she convinced herself that she was being truthful as she typed:

Hate to do this – got family business. Push to tomorrow? Promise. 2 o'clock tomorrow. THX 4 understanding.

Sam hit "send" but then thought, *Olga's dad is producing the new show, once I explain everything she'll totally understand about having to do pre-show publicity. Oh! He won't tell her about the show before I get the chance, will he? Nah – he's too busy to talk business with her.* That made her feel a little better, but then she thought of Carlos. He wasn't used to show business. What if he made the same assumption Rose did and thought her appointment with Seth was a date? Would he be upset? Would he get mad? Would he even care?

She headed down to breakfast, but as she flopped into a chair and grabbed a box of cereal, she realized that her stomach was a little queasy. *Probably nerves,* she said to herself. *I've got to chill.*

The rest of the morning was pretty mellow until her mom decided it was time to find Sam the perfect yoga outfit. Rose had Jean and Jehan at the ready; the moment she called for them, the wardrobe and hair and makeup brothers appeared seemingly out of nowhere and dismissed every T-shirt and pair of sweats Sam owned. In the end, they sent her off in some strange black leotard – with so many fancy straps around the back that Sam almost choked trying to put it on – and a pair of black dance pants that were uncomfortably tight around the waist. *I look like a walking licorice stick*, she said to herself as they messed with her hair and put shiny gloss on her lips.

Robert was waiting for her when she headed back downstairs.

"Remember," he said as they walked out toward the limo, "breathe, stay centered, and do what the instructor tells you. You don't need to show off or pull a muscle or break a bone. We start shooting in less than two weeks. The last thing I need is for you to hurt yourself and mess up our production schedule."

"Yeah," Sam said quietly. "Nice to know you care."

"Of course I care," he sniffed. "If we are going to rebrand you as a *real* star, you can't be seen looking foolish in public. Slings and casts scream *klutz* – not cute girl worth emulating. You have to work with me on this."

Emulating? Rebranding? Wasn't it just yesterday that he said she was the comic relief? Typical Robert. Sam's head began to hurt as much as her stomach from that too-tight waistband on those embarrassingly clingy black dance pants.

Rose rushed out to the limo and demanded one last look before Sam left. She stood back and beamed with pride. "You look beautiful, Sweetie." She almost started to cry. "I can't believe my baby is going out on her first date!"

"It's not a date, Mom!" Sam whined even louder than she had that morning. "It's an app—"

Sam caught Michi and Lou recording her from the other side of the limo and froze. Slowly she turned her head and glared at Robert. "Really? Is this necessary?"

Without saying a word, Robert pointed for her to get into the limo. Letting out a massive, disgruntled sigh, Sam did.

The ride to the yoga studio was very silent. Sam was beyond uncomfortable. The leotard kept riding up and the waistband was seriously digging in to her. With Michi and Lou recording the entire, awful time, she couldn't help getting angry as she imagined Blu watching the live feed from his office and laughing. *I'm so regretting this*, she thought. But then she remembered how hard her mom had worked to support her and Danni when they were little, teaching at the preschool, taking any smiling, friendly mom modeling gig she could get, and her anger faded fast. This may be embarrassing, but it was the least she could do.

Once they reached the studio, Sam stepped out, only to find a whole bunch of paparazzi filming Seth as he stood out front waiting for her.

"I'm so sorry," she said to him.

He put one arm around her and seemed to be trying to shield her from the photographers with the other.

Pulling his baseball cap down low to cover his mouth, he whispered back, "I tweeted one line of text about us taking a yoga class together and look at the response! Can you believe how interested they are? This is a good sign."

He hustled her into the studio before she could ask what he was talking about. There, he had two yoga mats waiting for them, right in the front of the room. Sam looked to see if they could move to the back, but the room was already filled with people, so she sat down and tried not to show how uncomfortable she was.

The class began and everything went okay for a while. Sam was enjoying the stretching, but then the teacher told everyone to stand so they could work on balance poses. Never known for being graceful, Sam was terrified that she'd fall over and end up knocking down a bunch more people in the process. Again, she was pleasantly surprised to find that the poses were kind of fun, until the teacher came over and whispered in her ear that her posture was off. She lifted Sam's head, pushed her hips forward, and used her hand to put pressure on Sam's tummy so she'd suck it in. That made something in Sam's stomach gurgle. The whole class heard it; a few people giggled. As if that wasn't enough, suddenly Sam really didn't feel so good. She felt gassy, shooting pains rumbled about in her gut. The pressure began to cause real pain, but the only way Sam could relieve it was either by burping or farting – neither of which was an option in a room full of people. It got so bad that she wanted to cry, but she managed to survive the class without any body gases escaping.

The very second the class was over, Sam raced out

of the room and headed for the limo. Seth was right next to her the whole way. As they exited the studio, the waiting photographers went crazy taking pictures and calling out to them. Again, Seth acted as if he was trying to protect Sam, but the way he was holding up his jacket still made it possible for all the paparazzi to get great shots of the two of them.

As they reached Sam's limo, Seth whispered in her ear, "That was awesome! You played it just right! I'm really going to enjoy working with you." Then, loud enough for all the paparazzi around them to hear, he said, "Yeah, I had fun too! I'll call you tonight." Then he hurried away to his own waiting limo.

Sam jumped in and slammed the door as fast as she could. Seeing that Robert wasn't in the back, she felt safe and alone and finally let go of the terrible gas that had been hurting so much. The fart was thunderous, but oh, did it feel good. Sitting back in her seat, Sam was horrified to glance up and see Michi and Lou, recording from the front. For a second, Sam hoped they wouldn't have noticed, but from the shaking of their bodies, it was more than obvious they knew exactly what had just happened.

Robert slipped into the limo from the street side. "How'd it go?" he asked.

Sam dropped her head. "Peachy. Just peachy."

"Great!" Robert didn't appear to have noticed Sam's body language or the sarcasm in her voice. "Then you'll be happy to hear that I just got a text from Seth's agent; you two will do lunch tomorrow."

"Me and Seth's agent?"

Robert stared at her blankly. "You and *Seth*," he replied.

The limo drove away with Sam remaining silent. It wasn't until they drove past the stables on their way back home that she remembered she'd already rain-checked Carlos and Olga for tomorrow.

When she tried to explain to Robert, he brushed off her concerns. "Listen, Samantha, this TV show is serious business. I'm sorry that you won't have as much time to go play with your friends, but there are a lot of people, including your mother, whose future paychecks depend on this show being a big success. There's a lot of competition for viewers out there and doing this kind of pre-show publicity will help get people interested enough to tune in to your show.

You either accept that or you quit now."

Sam wanted to tell Robert the whole deal was off, but as the limo pulled up in front of her home, she saw her mom was outside, waiting excitedly to hear all the details. Seeing her mom so happy burst Sam's resolve.

"Okay, okay. I'm in." She turned to face Robert, "But make sure that I'm home by two tomorrow, please? I'll go wherever you want for lunch, but I have to be home by two o'clock. Deal?"

Robert gave her a very serious nod of his head. "Deal."

Sam leaned across to open the limo door, but her mom had already raced over and opened it for her.

Rose was so busy asking questions, "How'd it go? Did you have fun? Was Seth nice? Did you enjoy the class?" that she practically dragged her daughter out of the limo and into the living room. After a solid thirty-minute interrogation, Sam managed to excuse herself and go up to her room.

She closed the bedroom door behind her and heard Blu's voice asking, "Is your tummy all better now or do I need to evacuate the area before you blow again?"

"Very funny." She walked over to the open control room and sat on the carpet right in front of it. "A real friend would show a little kindness and promise *never* to air that video."

Blu slid his chair over so he was looking down directly at Sam. "Relax," he said with a smile, "I won't use the footage, but *my-oh-my* was it entertaining. You didn't do that *in* the class, did you?"

"Nope." Sam shook her head before stopping and sitting up straight. "Oh! Michi and Lou didn't tape the class? How come?"

Blu rolled his eyes. "Seth and his agent weren't sure how well you'd do in the class and they didn't want to take a chance of *him* being seen in public with a klutz, meaning *you*. The kid has a *public persona* to protect. They wanted to be sure that the only video available was of him acting like a hero, protecting you from the big, bad paparazzi. Thus, we weren't allowed to set foot outside the limo, although we were strongly encouraged to get footage of him helping you in and out of it. Whatever."

"Oh. Yeah, whatever." Sam wasn't sure how to bring up the subject of the new TV show. She hoped

Blu would mention it first, but he didn't.

"So…?"

Blu studied Sam a moment. "Uh…so…what?"

Grunting in frustration that he wouldn't read her mind, she went ahead and asked, "Aren't you at all excited that we get to keep working together?"

With a confused expression, Blu replied with, "Huh?"

Sam grunted louder. "The new show? The one with me and Seth? Set at the stables, you're supposed to be the director, is any of this ringing a bell?"

Blu sat way back in his chair, clasped his hands behind his head, and pretended to act all nonchalant. "Oh *that* show? Yeah, it should be a nice little project."

Jabbing her fists into her hips, Sam snapped at him, "A nice little project? Blu! I fixed everything! You and I get to stay friends! Isn't that worth at least a *way-to-go* or *something* kind of congratulatory?"

It was Blu's turn to sit straight up. "Don't get upset; I'm teasing. This new adventure sounds exciting, but I have to be honest. I'm worried whether it's the right thing for you."

"What?" Sam was so surprised she almost fell over. "What's the problem?"

"How do I say this?" Blu rubbed his eyes before answering. "I've got a feeling that you're doing all this for the wrong reasons."

"Wanting to take care of my friends and family aren't right enough reasons?" she asked with a rather snarky expression on her face.

Blu took in a deep breath and pushed it out forcefully. "Chill, my friend, chill. Let's try this conversation again, *without* the major attitude."

Sam realized he was right. She bit her lip, slumped back, and waited.

Giving her an appreciative thumbs up, Blu continued. "As your *friend*, I'm thinking…my worry is…look, don't get me wrong, I'm not going to abandon you. I only agreed to direct the show so I could protect you as much as possible, but Sam, I'm begging you to give this a whole lot more thought because – whoops…"

Something on one of the monitors caught his eye. "Robert's on his way. Back up."

Sure enough, two seconds later, Robert knocked on Sam's door.

"Samantha," he said from the other side. "I need you to come downstairs so Jean and Jehan can begin getting all your measurements and mapping out your wardrobe."

Sam quietly answered, "Be right there."

Before standing, she took one last look in the mirror, "Don't worry, Blu," she said softly. "I know what I'm doing. Everything's going to be all right."

CHAPTER 9

Click click click, clack clack click.

Yesterday was freaky, but I have faith that today is going to be great! Why? Because despite having a horrible evening – getting poked and measured and color-charted for my new TV show (that sounds so wrong – *MY* TV show) – I got Robert to swear that I'd be home today in time to spend the whole afternoon with Olga and Carlos.

Besides, I'm having lunch with Seth (it's a meeting

– not a date!) at my favorite pizza place –
Minnicucci's. They make amazing pizzas and
the waiters sing great old Italian songs. It's tons
of fun.

I'll fill you in on all the details later. By the way, if
you ever go to Minnicucci's, order the meatball
special pizza. It's off-the-charts yummage!

Sam stepped out of the limo in front of Minnicucci's
and looked around for Seth, who was climbing out of
a limo that was parked further down the block.

"Hey, Sammy-girl," he called out as he walked
toward her – again wearing that same baseball cap.
"I waited in my car because I didn't want to cause a
scene."

There were few things in life Sam disliked more
than being called Sammy, and Sammy-girl sounded
even worse. But she knew she shouldn't say anything to
upset Seth, so she let it go.

They entered the restaurant and immediately
wonderful smells of fresh pizza sauce and baking dough
hit them.

"Oh, I love this place," she said as she inhaled the awesome scent.

"Yeah," Seth nodded half-heartedly, "it's sort of quaint."

The waiter offered them a table by the window, but Seth told him he preferred to sit in the back. "I don't want my quiet lunch to become a big paparazzi scene," he explained.

They sat down and looked over the menu.

"I don't know why I'm bothering to do this," Sam giggled. "I always order the meatball special pizza. It's my favorite."

Seth made a funky face. "Really? Do you know how many carbs are in one slice of pizza? You must have an amazing metabolism. I'm sticking to pure protein. How about trying the buffalo burger with me – with no bun of course. Everyone says it's the best."

Carbs? Protein? Sam, having never eaten buffalo, not understanding what Seth was worrying about, and really wanting her pizza, was about to say no. However, Robert's warning about them seriously needing Seth to get the show on TV popped into her head, so she stayed quiet, forced herself to smile, and nodded.

After ordering for the two of them, Seth pulled out his cell phone and set it on the table. "I hope this thing won't ruin our lunch," he said, "but I'm still waiting to hear about that car commercial so you'll understand if I need to answer it."

"Sure thing," Sam replied. "What kind of car is the commercial for?"

Seth shrugged. "Who knows? What's important is that the director and I really had a great video chat. The guy really seemed to like me."

Sam couldn't think of anything to say in response to that. She bit her lip as she struggled for something to get a conversation going.

"Um…so what did you do over the summer, Seth?" she asked as she tried to sip the sparkling water Seth had ordered for her. This wasn't as easy as it should have been. The bubbles in the water kept making the straw float up and out of the glass. After pushing it down several times, she gave up and set it on the table.

"It was great! I worked the whole time. I was in Canada shooting a movie and then flew to New York to be a host at a kids' award show; that was important because once people see you can handle yourself at some little awards show, they begin to think of you as a potential presenter or even as a host for the really important ones." He was eyeballing his cell phone while he talked. "Hey, I just got an important e-mail. You mind if I read it?"

Before Sam could answer, he'd lifted the phone and was scrolling away.

"I had a really mellow summer," she explained, trying to fill the stillness. "I hung out at the stables, read a ton of books, and watched a whole bunch of videos on YouTube."

"Yeah," Seth nodded but didn't look away from his cell phone, "YouTube rocks. There's a slew of interviews of me from the press junket I did for my Christmas movie last year."

"That's cool." Sam was pleased that Seth was at least listening to her – even if he was still keeping his eyes on his cell phone. "I was mostly watching old Muppet videos. They really cracked me up."

Seth shook his head as if something unpleasant had just woken him. With his face still pointing down toward his phone, he glanced up at her. "What'd you say? You watched the *Muppets*?"

"Yes." Seth's tone made Sam feel defensive. "It was a hoot to go back and watch all that stuff I liked so much as a little kid. Some of those skits and songs are even funnier now because…" Her voice trailed off until there was no sound at all, once Seth's eyes returned to his phone and it became super-obvious that he wasn't even pretending to listen anymore.

Trying to stay positive about the whole experience, Sam focused on the little machine in his hand. "I know that phone! That's a Blackberry. That's what Robert uses. He loves that thing!"

"Uh huh." Seth was nodding, but it was clear he hadn't heard a word.

The waiter brought the buffalo. Sam didn't hate it, but it definitely wasn't as good as her beloved meatball special. She looked out the window and saw a handful of people gathering outside the restaurant.

"I guess we got here just in time." She pointed. "There seems to be a crowd gathering."

Seth slowly turned his head just enough to glance outside. He quickly focused his attention back on Sam. "Don't look! It's the paparazzi. Keep your eyes on me."

"Uh…" Sam felt like a total goofball staring at Seth.

"Um…when I'm with my sister and the photographers show up, we usually sneak out the back." She swiveled in her chair to check out the back of the restaurant.

"No, don't do that!" Seth's voice was strong, but he kept a very charming grin on his face. "Keep looking at me and smiling. It's important they see us getting along."

The rest of the lunch was mega-mucho uncomfortable. Instead of talking to her, Seth continued giving her instructions on how to behave. By the time the meal was over, Sam was exhausted – and still hungry. Seth's directions had rarely included eating.

"Tell you what," he said as he made a big show of pulling out his wallet and handing his credit card to the waiter, "why don't you let me give you a lift back to your place. It'll look really great for us to leave in the same car."

Sam laughed. "But my limo is outside waiting. It seems like a total waste of gas for my car to follow us back to my house."

Seth stood up and held out his hand for Sam. "Come on, Sammy-girl. I know I wasn't a lot of fun to talk to today. Sorry about that. I'm hardcore focused on that commercial. Let me give you a ride home. I promise I'll be more entertaining."

No boy had ever held his hand out to Sam like that before. She was beyond surprised, then she got all embarrassed. Slowly she reached out and put her hand inside Seth's.

"Okay," she managed to squeak. "I'm in."

With Seth leading the way, the two weaved and bobbed through the photographers outside the restaurant. Sam giggled the whole time; it was too silly, but it was also kind of fun having Seth act so protective – as if he really liked her – *liked her* liked her. However, the minute they got in and closed the limo door, Seth settled into his seat and focused his attention on his Blackberry.

Sighing, Sam buckled her seat belt and thought about how much she missed her iPhone. She'd left it on the windowsill in her room, hoping it would dry out. Maybe it would be working by now. She'd check it as soon as she got home.

Home! Sam panicked. Without her cell phone she didn't know what time it was. Olga and Carlos were going to be at her house around two o' clock.

"Seth, what time is it?" she asked.

He didn't answer.

"Seth?"

Still nothing.

"Excuse me, Mr. Driver," she called out to the chauffeur. "What time is it, please?"

"It's five minutes to two, Miss Devine."

Sam flinched. The last thing she wanted was for her friends to be sitting around her house waiting for her. "Excuse me, sir," she called out again. "I don't mean to be pushy or anything, but if you could drive super-fast, I'd *really* appreciate it."

The driver nodded. "Tighten your seat belt, Miss. This could be a bumpy ride."

And, indeed, it was, but Sam loved it. *This is so the highlight of my day so far*, she thought as the limo swung hard around a tight corner and raced up the street toward her house. As it pulled into her driveway, she saw Carlos and Olga getting off their bikes.

Whoo, she sighed with relief, *I'm not late. They haven't been waiting*.

Sam was so excited to see her friends she opened the door while the limo was still moving.

"Slow your roll, girl!" Seth said as she hopped out.

"Howdy! Howdy!" Sam bounced over to her friends. She was so happy to see them that she didn't notice Seth stepping out and walking over, but Olga and Carlos did.

"Hey there," Seth said coolly as he adjusted the brim of his baseball cap.

Sam had forgotten all about him and was genuinely surprised to find him standing right next to her. However, out of the corner of her eye, she noticed Michi and Lou heading toward them with their full audio and video gear ready for action and immediately Sam understood why Seth had bothered getting out of the limo.

Seth waited for the crew to get close before extending his hand coolly to Carlos. "Hey man. Seth Black. You are…?"

Carlos shook hands and replied, "Carlos Victorio. This is my cousin Olga."

"Victorio?" Seth warmed up. "You related to our producer, Caesar Victorio?"

"That's my dad," Olga replied proudly.

Seth's entire face exploded with his super-charming

smile. "So *you're* Olga Victorio! Your father mentioned you when we met last week to discuss my—" he paused before motioning to Sam, "*our* new TV show. He said you loved my last movie." He touched the brim of his baseball cap again. "Would you like an autographed hat from it? I have several in the trunk."

"Uh…" Olga looked rather uneasy. "I suppose my sister would."

"Great!" Seth spun around and returned in less than a minute with another baseball cap and a marker. "What's her name?"

"Inga," Sam, Carlos, and Olga all answered at the same time.

The three looked at each other for a moment before cracking up.

"Jinx!" Olga called out. "Now neither one of you can talk until I say your names."

Seth was too busy writing on the cap to hear any of this. When he finished, he held it up and read it out loud, "To Inga, thanks for being such an awesome fan. Stay rockin' and listen to your dad. Seth Black." He handed the hat to Olga and turned to Sam.

"Today rocked. My agent thought it would be

great if for our next lunch we went out for sushi. You in?"

Seeing as Sam was under the power of *jinx*, she couldn't speak, making it tough to explain that she'd never had sushi before, but it sounded pretty gross. Keeping her lips firmly glued together, she sort of shrugged and moved her head around.

Seth stared at her as if she'd lost her mind. "Hmm… I'll take that as a *yes*. See you soon, Sammy-girl! Ciao everyone."

As his limo drove away, Olga turned to Sam and in total disbelief asked, "*Sammy-girl?*"

Sam shook her head and covered her mouth with her hands.

Olga sighed. "Oh, I get it. Sam – there you're officially unjinxed. Okay – *Sammy-girl*. What is this all about?"

Walking toward the house, Sam tried to brush off the topic. "It's kind of a long story. Let's go hang by the pool and I'll explain."

"No way." Olga stood her ground. "Listen, I was really hurt when you didn't tell me yourself about this whole TV show thing." Seeing the stunned expression on Sam's face, Olga nodded. "Yeah, it was hardly fun finding out *from Inga* that my best friend was going to become a TV star, and keep her reality show in a way very close to the idea *I* came up with, but I let that go. Then you go and blow off Carlos and me. Not cool, still, it happens, okay. However – letting that little twerp get away with calling you a totally lame – *ohh we're so tight* – nickname like that? It's *so* not you."

Ashamed to meet her friend's eyes, Sam glanced over at Carlos. His face was blank. She couldn't tell what he was thinking.

"Olga, it's...it's complicated," Sam stammered. "Robert says we need him for the show so I have to keep him happy. It's all just pre-show publicity. Come on," she gestured toward the front door, "I'm seriously sorry I didn't tell you about the show myself; I didn't know how. Too much is happening too fast. I just need some *hang out and be normal time*. Let's forget all about this for now, okay, please? It's really nothing."

Olga put her hands on her hips. "It's *not* nothing. I just heard Seth say you're going out for sushi. Are you *dating* that doorknob?"

Feeling total mortification at the thought of

Carlos thinking she'd been on a date, Sam got defensive. "It wasn't a date. Seth is my co-star and I have to get along with him. Please don't call him a doorknob."

"But he *is* a doorknob!" Olga wailed. "I can't believe you canceled on us yesterday to go to some yoga class with that gerbil!" Seeing the stunned expression on Sam's face, Olga nodded. "Yes, I know about that too – pictures of you guys are all over the internet. I *get* that you have to be friends since you're going to work together, but…acting all *mushy* and *coupley* with him? Eww! And that whole thing – just now – about him *pretending* to know who I am because of my dad? What a fake! My dad would never talk about me in a business meeting. The only reason that little creep was trying to make all nicey-nice with me is because as the producer of—" Olga held up her hands and made air quotes, "'*his show*', my dad is *his* boss." She shook her head. "He's a worm and he's only pretending to like you so you'll be happy playing second fiddle to him in that dumb show."

Sam's jaw dropped. "*What?*"

"You heard me." Olga folded her arms in front of herself. "It's a dumb show, taking over *The Devine Life* is a dumb idea, and you should quit everything right now!"

"Olga Victorio," Sam whispered hoarsely through quivering lips. "You take that back."

"I will not." Olga dug in her heels. "You need to hear me out; I'm your best friend. I've always told you the truth. I know you're dealing with a ton of craziness. You've got Danni leaving, you're worried about your mom, you're worried about this house, but Sam, you are thirteen years old! It's not your job to carry the weight of the world and try to be everybody's hero. Look at you, you're totally tied in knots after just a couple of days of being *Sammy-girl*."

Fighting back tears, Sam whispered, "You don't get it."

"Yes I do!" Olga threw her arms in the air. "It's you that doesn't get it! Haven't you learned anything from your sister? Poor Danni is wound up tighter than a cuckoo clock! Her big dream is to walk away from all the showbiz baloney that you are running into head first! And the cherry on top of this sundae is you dating Mr. *Hey-Everybody-Look-At-Me*! Don't you see that he's exactly the kind of person you've been trying to avoid since your sister became famous?"

Sam pulled on her hair. "I'm not dating Seth! It wasn't a date! It was an appointment! Yes, the guy's got a big ego, but I'm stuck with him. I need you to understand!" She looked at Carlos. "Please. I need both of you to understand. I'm doing all of this to take care of my mom! I don't like Seth Black! I am not dating Seth Black!"

At that moment, Rose opened the door and clasped her hands to her chest. "You're home! How was your date?"

Sam let out a major, "*Aurgh!*" and ran up to her room.

She sat alone on the edge of her bed for a good twenty minutes before her mom knocked on her door.

"Sweetie," Rose called out gently. "I think we need to talk."

Sam didn't answer, but Rose walked in anyway. She sat next to her daughter.

"Olga gave me a quick version of what happened. Guess I should get an award for great moments in bad timing, eh?"

In spite of herself, Sam snorted a tiny laugh, but it was followed by a big whine.

"I'm just trying to do right by everybody, Mom, really I am. Robert told me to keep Seth happy because if he bails, then we lose the show. Why is Olga being so harsh about all this?"

Putting her arm around Sam, Rose gave her a little hug. "Honey, she's not being harsh. She's just afraid that she's losing her best friend."

"Oh please." Sam shook her head. "I put her off for one day and she makes this big deal about it. That's lame."

"It's not the *one day*, Sam. Remember, Olga's grown up around show business. She's seen lots of people change in order to become or stay famous. How many times have the two of you sat in the living room and made fun of Danni for acting silly or snooty around other famous people or on some talk show? I've heard you girls laughing your heads off at little Inga for pandering to every celebrity she meets, and from Olga's point of view, you appear to be doing the very same thing."

Sam didn't respond.

"You can understand how difficult it must be for her to see you getting swept away with a million new responsibilities that will keep the two of you apart." Rose tried to hide a tiny grin as she continued, "And let's not forget, she is Carlos's cousin. She doesn't want to see him get his heart broken."

An electric shock jolted Sam's body. She stared at her mom in stunned silence.

Rose tried hard to hide her amusement at Sam's reaction. "Don't act all surprised. Of course I know you like Carlos and it's plain he likes you too. You think I'm *too old* to notice that kind of thing? Give me a little credit, will ya?"

Shifting her weight so she could face her daughter, Rose tapped Sam on the chin. "You need to tell me what you want. If this TV show is too much for you, say the word and I'll make it all go away. But if you do want it, you have to be willing to put in the extra time and effort to stay true to yourself and the people you love," she grinned, "and any person you like…a lot…as more than a friend…maybe even as a boyfr—"

"*Don't* say that word." Sam held up her hand. It was weird enough having her mom talk about Carlos, but to hear her use the *boyfriend* word was more than she could handle.

Rose smoothed Sam's hair. "All right. I can see you've had enough for one day, but if you ever do want to discuss boys and—"

"*Mom!*" Sam wailed. "I got it." She stood up and paced for a bit before saying, "And I do get what you're saying about my friends, but let me deal with this on my own, okay?"

"Okay." Rose stood up. "Might as well start dealing now. I heard Olga say something to Carlos about going to the stables." She put her hand in her pocket. "Want some money to maybe hang out there and grab some dinner?"

Sam started to reach out her hand, but pulled it back. "Nah, it's cool. For something like this, I think it'd be better if I used my allowance. It just seems more *right*. Does that sound silly?"

"Not at all." Rose beamed. "It seems very mature and very much like the Sam Devine we all know and love."

As her mom left the room, Sam remembered she'd wanted to check her iPhone to see if it had dried out.

Plugging it in, she gritted her teeth and thought, *Come on, baby, you can do it! Work! Work!*

To her delight, it began powering up and only a minute later, it appeared to be as good as new. She hit the "text" button and began typing:

Sorry (x 4ever) 4 everything! Seth = 8-(

U r my BFF – 4reals!!! We ok?

Sam squinched her eyes shut and held her breath as she hit "send" and waited for a reply. The ten seconds it took for one to come was agony. When she heard the tiny "ding" signaling she had a message, Sam carefully peeled her eyes open and read:

Sorry 2!! All good!! Come hang @ SuAn!

Typing as she walked, which meant almost tumbling down the stairs, Sam somehow managed to stay upright, as she happily replied:

C u in 2!

CHAPTER 10

Sam came home from the stables happy, sweaty, and seriously smelly. Her late afternoon ride with Olga was total bliss. They talked and laughed and had a wonderful time.

The minute she walked back into the house her mom sent her up for a shower with a warning that as soon as she was clean, she needed to get to work learning her lines for the rehearsal early the next morning. Even the thought of everything she needed to get done before going to bed that night couldn't ruin her great mood.

After getting all clean, she threw on a pair of

sweatpants and headed downstairs to sneak a pre-dinner snack, but on her way to the kitchen, the doorbell rang.

"I'll get it," she yelled, changing direction.

Upon opening it, she found herself facing a very nice-looking man.

"Sam," he said warmly. "I've been looking forward to meeting you." He extended his hand to shake hers. "It's going to be a pleasure working with you."

"Um…okay," she replied as she slowly extended her hand. "I…I…" she looked at him blankly, "I suppose I'd feel the same way if I knew who you were."

The man smiled. "Ah – I guess I'm a surprise? No worries. I'm Mr. Daniels, your studio teacher."

"Oh, my studio teacher." Sam nodded and smiled back before shaking her head. "I don't know what that means."

The man laughed good-naturedly. "Well, either you are Samantha Devine, star of the upcoming family show and I'm going to be your tutor for the next year, or I'm at the wrong house and annoying an innocent bystander."

Tutor? But school was supposed to start next week!

Rose's voice rang out from behind Sam. "Oh, honey, I thought Robert explained this to you yesterday." She walked over and placed her hands gently on her daughter's shoulders. "The only way we can get enough episodes of your show shot before you go through any growth spurts is to shoot straight through the whole year. There's no way you can attend regular school with that schedule. Mr. Daniels will be on set with you every day to ensure you get the required amount of schooling in."

Sam was so surprised by the news that she stood there completely dumbfounded while Rose and Mr. Daniels introduced themselves to each other. Tutor? On the set? Every day? School was such a natural part of life that she hadn't even considered how being in a real TV show would cause a conflict.

"But, but Mom," she stammered. "I'm going to Middle School! This is the first year that we have sports teams and stuff. I wanted to see about being on the school newspaper and the yearbook committee."

Rose gently smoothed Sam's hair. "Oh, Little Bit, there's no way you'll have time for any of that – not with all your commitments to the show. Those things will all be around in another couple of years when you complete your show's run. Trust me, it'll be wonderful having all the one-on-one attention of your very own tutor."

With a demure smile and a batting of her eyelashes, Rose invited Mr. Daniels in, offered him a *beverage*, and asked if he'd like *the grand tour*. That greatly annoyed Sam. They lived in a big house and had a nice backyard, but it wasn't exactly a *museum*. And why was her mom being so girly and chatty with this teacher dude? As the adults walked away, leaving Sam alone at the front door, she found herself feeling seriously grumpy, but why?

As she closed the front door, Sam heard the text alarm ding on her cell phone. Her heart skipped a beat when she saw that it was from Carlos:

Sorry to have missed you at the stables. Finishing paperwork to begin my schooling this fall. See you soon – I hope. Carlos

Sam giggled. How awesome that he was thinking of her! Plus, how totally adorable that he didn't know how to use short text language to communicate on a cell phone – at least not in English. Having Carlos around really was awesome. Sitting at the bottom of the big staircase, Sam had a flash of understanding. Rose had been flirting with Mr. Daniels! Danni was the queen of flirting – Sam had seen her do it a million times – but she'd never seen her mom do it before. Right away Sam felt guilty. Here she was, enjoying the excitement of her first crush, but getting tweaked at her mom for acting like she had an eye for Mr. Daniels.

"Man oh man," she said out loud, "I really am a selfish butthead sometimes."

Pulling herself up, she headed to the kitchen for that snack and noticed Mr. Daniels and her mom sitting outside on the chairs by the pool. Sam giggled as she saw her mom tilt her head toward Mr. Daniels whenever she laughed and how his smile widened when she reached out her hand to lightly touch his shoulder. Even though Sam felt badly about spying on her mom, she couldn't tear herself away.

After some time, Danni walked into the kitchen.

"What's with the big grin?" she asked as she walked over next to her sister. "Who's that guy with Mom?"

"That's my new tutor," Sam explained while

keeping her eyes fixed on the scene playing out by the pool.

"Huh," Danni set down her shopping bags and watched along with Sam. "He's a good-looking guy. Mom sure seems to be enjoying herself. It's about time."

Sam looked up at Danni. "What does that mean?"

"It means that in all the time Mom has been a widow, she's never once had a date or gone out to dinner with a man just for the fun of it. She's always been so focused on taking care of you and me that she's never gone and gotten a life for herself. I think this is pretty cool." Danni turned away and walked over to the refrigerator. She opened a bottle of water before adding, "Mom must be feeling pretty secure with life now that I'm grown-up and moving out and you're become a star in your own right."

Seeing her sister finally relaxed and more like her normal self, Sam thought this was a good time to ask her some specifics about all the pressures and drama that went into being a star. It was one thing to spend the last two years experiencing a little of what being famous was like, but actually being the center of attention was turning out to be completely different.

"Danni," she asked gingerly, "do you think I'm making a mistake?"

Danni froze mid-drink. She slowly lowered the bottle from her lips and stared at her sister. "Do you *not* want to do this, Sam? I was told you were one hundred percent gung-ho about being in your own show. If you aren't you need to say something now! Being in show business is a way of life not a little side gig. It's a ton of work. No one understands that until they are smack in the middle of it, because most people only see the cool stuff – the fancy clothes, the travel, the big parties. You do get wicked amazing rewards, but you give up a major piece of your life rehearsing, practicing how to speak in public and getting all dressed up to go out no matter the time of day, because you can't be seen looking like a ragamuffin who just rolled out of bed. Somebody once told me there's some tribe from…somewhere…? I don't know. Anyway, these people believe that if you take a person's picture, you take away a piece of their soul. Sometimes it really starts feeling that way. It's as if you have to give up a billion tiny pieces of your soul and pass them out for a bunch of strangers to examine and judge. Then when they get bored with the first billion pieces, they demand a billion more. If you don't want to be a star with all your heart you have to bail immediately! There are too many people involved. Too many people, whose financial futures depend on your success, for you to get started and then decide to quit before everyone who has invested time and money in you has a chance to get it all back and then some."

Danni's serious expression truly spooked Sam. She wasn't used to her sister being so straightforward and businesslike with her.

"Oh no." She forced herself to shake her head. "I'm not thinking that way at all. I understand everything you're saying. I'm into this for me. I really want to be a big star."

"Then I wish you the best fortune in the whole wide world," Danni exclaimed as she hugged her little sis. "And now, I'm going back up to my room to look at paint chips. I still can't decide if I want the guest bathroom to be apple green or honeydew."

Sam stuck our her tongue. "Ew, no matter what you choose, it sounds gross to be thinking about a bathroom color that's connected with food."

Laughing, Danni picked up her bags and glanced out the window one last time. "Hmm…Mom really seems to be enjoying her time with your tutor guy. I always figured she and Robert would eventually end up together, but this is way more cool."

As Danni left the kitchen, Sam's jaw hit the ground. Never in a gazillion years had she *ever* thought of Robert and her mom… *Going out? Dating? Getting married?!* An involuntary shudder ran through Sam's body. Robert Ruebens as her stepfather? The very idea was not just revolting, it was so hilarious that Sam laughed out loud.

"Care to share what's so darn funny?" a voice shot out from behind her.

Spinning around faster than a feather in a hurricane, Sam was mortified to see Robert entering the kitchen. Had she said anything incriminating out loud? She tried desperately to figure out if she had any reason to be embarrassed.

It didn't appear that she did as Robert set his briefcase on the kitchen counter and began messing with a strange, flat electronic thing. He pulled out a bunch of wires, plugged one thing into another and handed Sam a thick pen that attached to the machine.

"Here," he said. "I need you to carefully sign your name on this tablet."

"Why? What is that?"

Robert shook the pen again for Sam to take. "It's a digi-pen. Once we have your signature digitized, you won't have to worry about signing any fan mail. We can connect this to a big computer and all your *thanks for writing and please keep watching the show* letters will be automatically signed and sent with a photo personally autographed by you."

Sam remembered the scene with Danni over her digitized signature, way back at the start of this whole dramatic chapter of her life. Her first reaction was to giggle at the thought of receiving fan mail. Her second was to argue with Robert that, if her signature was coming from a computer rather than her own hand, it wasn't real and shouldn't count as something *personally autographed*. But then she remembered she needed to keep Robert busy and away from Rose and Mr. Daniels so they could continue enjoying their time together. Adding Robert to the mix was a surefire way to ruin the romantic moment. So she bounced over, took the pen, and began carefully signing her name on the fancy machine.

"Okay, done," she said, handing back the pen. "Thanks for coming. See you tomorrow."

Totally missing her cue for him to leave, Robert handed Sam a large, hardcover book before absent-mindedly poking his head into the pantry, pulling out a box of crackers, and starting to munch his way through them. Sam put the book on the counter, folded her arms, and tapped her foot, waiting for him to realize that his work was done. Instead, Robert, talking with his mouth full of crackers, pointed at the book, "That's your brand book. Learn it; live it."

"My what?"

Robert chewed furiously for a moment to try and clear the dry crackers from his mouth. "Your *brand book*. Go through all the pictures. From this point forward, that dictates what clothes you wear, what soda you drink, and what candy you need to be seen eating, things like that."

Sam flipped through the pages. "You are seriously kidding, right?" She pointed at a page with two different kinds of soft drinks pictured. "I don't drink that stuff. I like orange cream soda."

"Not anymore you don't," Robert answered without looking at her. He was busy trying to brush all the crumbs off his suit coat. "It's especially important with you as the focus of *The Devine Life*. Study that book very carefully and begin making changes immediately. Now that you're becoming a *real* celebrity, we need to be sure you maintain a carefully crafted image that matches all the marketing deals we've made for you. Oh, that reminds, me...where's your mother?"

Sam felt certain her mom's first attempt at a social life wasn't any of Robert's business. She worried, too, that Danni might have been onto something and perhaps Robert would get jealous, seeing Rose with another man. Then, what if Robert saw Mr. Daniels and suddenly felt compelled to spring into action and declare his love for Rose? That would be awful! Sam could live with the guy as her *agent*, but not as her *stepfather*. *Bother, bother bother,* she thought, *as if my life wasn't complicated enough!* She tried to change the subject.

"Why...why are you asking? Hey, I'll read the book, right now. Look, Robert, I'm picking up the book to go upstairs and memorize it this very instant. You can leave now, I'm getting right to work."

Robert appeared rather pleased with that response. "Good answer! I like your enthusiasm. But I still need to talk to your mother. She hasn't been answering her cell phone. I need her to sign some documents on the extension of your contract with the network and—"

Sam saw Robert notice Rose and Mr. Daniels out by the pool. She saw that the sight surprised him enough to stop talking – at least for a couple of seconds.

Still holding the box of crackers, Robert carefully moved closer to the glass door to get a better look.

"Who is your mother talking to?" he asked.

"Nobody special," Sam said in a light, chipper voice. "It's just my new tutor, Mr. Daniels. You're the one who hired him, aren't you?"

Without taking his eyes away from the scene outside, Robert replied, "I hired a tutor through an agency. I never met the person. I'm a little surprised by this; I assumed it would be a woman."

Sam slapped her hand on the kitchen counter to try and pull Robert's focus onto her. "Ha! That's so funny! You're really funny, Robert!"

But Robert didn't look at Sam, he kept his focus squarely on the two people still laughing and chatting animatedly. Slowly he set down the box of crackers, straightened his tie, and walked outside.

Sam raced upstairs to Danni's room. This weird world of grown-up stuff was beyond her understanding. She needed help figuring out how best to deal with this new complication. But when she flung open her sister's door, the light was off and the snoring was at full volume. Annoyed to the hilt, Sam hustled back to her room to call Olga.

CHAPTER 11

Click click click, clack clack click.

A bazillion apologies I haven't written in so long; actually it's only been a week – but it's been *a crazy one!* In fact, right now it's 5:30 a.m – the sun isn't even up yet – and this is seriously the first moment I've had in seven whole days to sit and blog. See, I've had to balance spending time with Seth, learning my lines for the show (which seem to change every fifteen minutes – what is UP with those writers, can't they make up their minds???), costume fittings, makeup and lighting tests, and doing interviews (they stuck me in a hotel room and I had to spend one *whole day* answering *the SAME QUESTIONS* over and over again to about thirty different reporters – it was insane)! I don't know when the *glamorous* part of showbiz begins, but I can tell you, the *work till you're about to drop* part starts right away and doesn't seem to let up EVER!

This is my life right now – I'm up, in my room, alone (well *duh* – it is 5:30, no wait – now it's 5:36 in the morning and no normal person is awake). I'm supposed to be going over my lines for today's rehearsals, but I just can't. I'm so sick of memorizing. It's all I do now – memorize words someone else has written and then try to say those words while doing blocking (moving from spot to spot) that someone else has worked out for me (okay – my character). This is very frustrating; I want to be a great *writer* – not a world-class memorizer! And what makes this even more frustrating is that the only thing I seem ever to truly remember is what having *fun was* like. Every time I ask for some free time, the answer is always *"No, Sam, because…"*

That should be the new title for *The Devine Life*, *The No, Sam, Because Show*.

No, Sam, you can't go get pizza with Olga and Carlos because….

No, Sam, you can't go riding this afternoon because…

No, Sam, you can't go to school and be normal because…

You get the picture.

Well, tonight, I'm taking matters into my own hands to get some of that precious *me* time back!

See, something major occurred that I HAVE to tell you about. Last week my *private tutor,* Mr. Daniels,

came to the house to say hello: no school for me this year — freaky, eh?

Anyway, my mom and Mr. Daniels totally connected; they spent a major part of the evening talking and laughing.

Robert came over, saw this, and *beelined* out to them and then basically *immediately*, both Mr. Daniels and Robert left. Mind you, there was no drama, but it all just seemed kind of...I don't know...*off*.

I called Olga right away and she thought this was the most awesome thing ever! It seems she agrees with Danni that Robert has some kind of unpronounced love for my mom! My response to this — *BLECH*!

Carlos said once that Olga watches too many romance movies, and he may have a point, but let me tell you, when my best friend is convinced she's right about something — she usually *is* right

(YIKES!) The more I told her she was crazy, the more she wigged me out with a ton of reasons *why* she was right. This has me massively worried. I can't have Mom and Robert getting involved! The thought of it makes my stomach spin like a blender in a milkshake shop.

Thus, after careful consideration, I have decided to take matters into my own hands and ensure that my name never becomes Samantha Sue Ruebens!

I call my plan *Operation Cupid.*

I've been carefully laying the groundwork for this with little comments and questions to Mom and Mr. D all week and tonight the *third act* (that's TV speak for the *big action*) is a *go*!

While I'm on the set today, I'm going to mention to Mr. Daniels how confused I am about something academic (trust me – considering how fried my brain is these days, it won't be hard to find something I need extra assistance understanding). Then I'm going to invite Mr. D over for dinner so he can help me AND I'll be sure to mention that I'd already discussed this with Mom and she thought it was an excellent idea.

Next, when I do finally get home from *another* long day of rehearsals and fittings and whatever other baloney they need me to do for the show today, Olga and Carlos will come over to help me get everything ready for the perfect romantic dinner. Over dinner, Mom and Mr. Daniels can cement their attraction, officially become a couple, and ensure that the Devine family bloodline remains *Ruebens-free*.

This is going to work; it has to. And just so you don't think I'm totally heartless, if I truly believed there was going to be some kind of big romance between my mom and Robert, I'd have some serious emotional baggage to sift through, but I'd find a way to deal with it. My goal is not to ruin what could be between Mom and Robert, but to cement what *should* be between Mom and Mr. D (did I mention how much I enjoy being tutored by him?) It would be wicked cool to have someone as nice and smart as Mr. Daniels sitting next to Mom at our family meetings.

Sam stopped typing. When had the last family meeting been? Only a week ago – yet things were spinning so fast, it felt as if it had been months. She yawned, stared over at the script she was *supposed* to have memorized by rehearsal today, and thought. Starring in her own TV show should have been her ticket to keeping her world together – but she was now so crazy busy, she barely had time to *be* in her world anymore. There had been no family meetings or family breakfasts, or family anythings, all week. With rehearsals starting so early, a real breakfast was out of the question; Sam ended up scarfing down a hunk of cheese and an apple in the limo. Lunch was eaten in her trailer while she went over her lines. Then she had her school time with Mr. D, and in the limo coming home, Sam usually ended up giving a couple more telephone interviews.

Dinners were either some meeting with a sponsor of the show or another super-strange outing with Seth. What was up with that guy? On the set, he barely spoke to her outside of rehearsals, but in public he acted as if she was the most important person in his life.

Only a week ago, Sam had believed that stepping into Danni's shoes as a star would solve her biggest worries, but now she had a whole new slew of issues and desperately needed things to slow down so she could breathe, but there was no room for that apparently. The frustration of it made her head hurt. She threw the script on the floor, leaned forward and gently tapped on one of the tiny microphones hidden by her computer desk.

"Blu?" she whispered. "Blu? You there? I really need to talk."

There was no answer.

"Please, Blu," she begged. "If you are there, I'm dying over here! Please talk to me!"

Realizing it was silly to expect Blu to be working at that crazy hour of the morning, Sam sighed and turned back to her blog.

Just looked at the clock — it's 5:42 a.m. and the limo will be here at 6:00. I've got just enough time to finish getting ready and grab another apple and a hunk of cheese to eat on the way to the set as I cram the last of my lines for today.

Gotta tell ya — I'm really getting sick of apples and cheese.

Twelve hours later, Sam sat impatiently on the front steps of her house, tapping her toes, waiting for Olga and Carlos to arrive with the ingredients that would ensure Operation Cupid's success. As she went over every detail in her mind, she was lost so deeply in thought that she didn't see Michi and Lou walking toward her. It wasn't until Lou accidently kicked a pebble from the driveway into Sam's field of vision that she was startled enough to look up and see them. Her tiny smile of acknowledgement turned into a huge grin once they got close enough for Sam to stare up into the camera lens.

"Hey, Blu," she whispered. "May I speak to you for a minute?"

Michi shook the camera, "No."

"Aww, come on! Please?" Sam begged.

Michi pulled out her earpiece and handed it to Sam who quickly held it up to her own ear.

"Yeah! Thanks!"

"Make it quick," Blu's voice growled in her ear. "You know this is a huge breach of protocol."

"Okay. Here's the thing, you know all about my plan tonight. You've heard me discussing it on the phone with Olga, right?"

"Yes, Sam," Blu's voice softened into brotherly annoyance. "I know all about *Operation Cupid*."

"Great!" Sam was relieved she didn't have to go into any of the details since her time with Blu was so brief. "What do you think? It's pretty brilliant, isn't it? I'm doing the right thing trying to help out my mom with her sad state of a social life, right?"

"That's a nice way to spin it," Blu replied. "But we both know you're doing this as much for yourself as for her."

"That's kind of cold," Sam pouted.

Blu chuckled. "It's not cold. It's the truth. Look, I think it's really cute how you put so much thought and effort into this dinner tonight, but at least be honest with yourself. It's also a little selfish. You want to be sure that your mom *doesn't* get involved with Robert just as much as you hope she *does* get involved with your tutor. My honest opinion is you shouldn't go messing with other people's love lives. How would you like it if your Mom interfered with you and Carlos?"

Sam cringed. "*Ouch.*"

"My point exactly. Listen, you've been working hard, you deserve a fun diversion. Go ahead with this *Operation*, but don't take this all so seriously. You're only thirteen; you should be enjoying this time, not trying to fix every problem for every person in your world."

Sam snorted, "You sound like Olga."

Blu laughed. "Considering that I think that girl is *good folk*, I'll take that as a compliment. And I hope you'll take my advice. Chill out. Be a goofy teenager. Stop taking everything so seriously. You really do need to have more fun or you're going to have a nervous breakdown before you turn fifteen."

Sam felt a bit stung by Blu's words, but somehow they were comforting too. "Sometimes I forget that you're not my own age," she said with a wry smile, "but then you say something super-smart like that and I remember how only *old* people can be so wise."

Giggling at her own joke, Sam didn't hear Blu's initial response and had to ask, "Huh? What did you say?"

"I said, ha, ha – very funny, and then asked you to give me your undivided attention for one more minute. There's something I need to tell you, and need you to be cool about it."

Sam nodded and motioned zipping her lips closed.

"Next Sunday evening, the night before we begin shooting your new show, that will be the end of my tenure as your secret-stuck-in-the-control-room friend slash reality show director."

"What?" she practically shouted.

"I thought I could handle both jobs, but it's too much work for one person," Blu replied. "I can only focus on one show at a time and I think it's best I go with the new one. Michi is going to take over as the director of *The Devine Life*. So – rather than freaking you out and getting you all upset – I thought I'd give you the news now and make sure you're prepared when it becomes official."

Sam gulped so hard she choked and coughed.

"Sam?" Blu sounded seriously worried. "You all right?"

"But, but," she blubbed. "But I thought that by doing the stables show I'd get to keep you! This isn't what I wanted!"

"Hey now. Come on, get a grip." Blu's voice was sincere and understanding. "I'm not abandoning you. I'm going to be there on-set with you every day. We'll be able to talk any time you want. And with Michi as your director for the reality show, everything will be great. You already know her and trust her, right?"

Meekly Sam answered, "Yeah."

"It's going to work out. Michi's got some fresh ideas about updating the look and feel of *The Devine Life*. She's going to move the hidden cameras around the house and make life even better for you. I promise."

Raising her hand to cover her mouth, Sam whispered, "Does she know about our deal where you never show footage of me sneaking orange cream soda in my room?"

Blu laughed so hard at that comment he began to cough and choke. "Yes, she does. It's all cool."

"Then...I guess it's okay."

"Good! Now hand her back the earpiece. I see the Victorio's car pulling up the driveway."

Sam handed the earpiece back to Michi. "Congrats on your promotion," she said.

Michi smiled broadly and gave Sam a big thumbs up before stepping back to film Olga and Carlos getting out of the car.

The three friends quickly discovered that carrying loads of stuff from the front door to the kitchen without getting caught wasn't easy. Yet, somehow, they managed to do it.

"Why is your mom still here?" Olga asked in a hushed voice. "I thought she was supposed to be out until dinner time."

Sam held up her iPhone. "My diversion is running behind schedule but I just sent a text that should get this brilliant plan back on track."

A moment later, Danni could be heard yelling.

"Mom! I broke a nail! Will you come with me to the salon to get it fixed? I'm at the front door all ready to go. Mom? Hey, Mom! Come on, Mom! My treat! Let's go."

Rose's voice boomed out from the intercom. "For heaven's sake, Dannielle Ann!"

Sam had to put both hands over her mouth to keep from laughing as she pictured her mother's irritated face. Danni's scream had been obnoxious, but it did the trick. Hearing her mom's high heels clicking on the marble floor as she scurried over to her eldest daughter's side gave Sam a huge rush of relief. *Talk about a win-win situation*, Sam thought as she gave herself a mental pat on the back, *not only will Mom feel extra pretty at dinner tonight, but she'll be in an especially good mood after having a little mother–daughter time with Danni.*

Carlos and Olga unloaded the bags. The entire kitchen counter was covered with fresh veggies, expensive cheeses, fancy breads, and a bunch of different bottles of wine.

"Why so much vino?" Sam asked. "Hold on, how did you guys get this wine?"

Carlos smiled. "I broke the rules and explained our plan to Uncle Caesar this morning. When we got home from school today he handed me all these bottles and said if it gets your mom to relax even a little, it's worth the investment."

Olga was washing lettuce in the sink. "It's too true," she laughed. "Dad's been getting really fed up with Robert's never-ending phone calls, faxes, and e-mails about things your mom is freaking out about. We really are doing a good thing here, Sam – your mom seriously needs to get a life."

As she pulled out Rose's good china, Sam thought that despite Blu's warning not to take this plan too seriously, maybe something good could come out of the dinner, aside from Sam getting to spend some desperately needed time with Olga and Carlos. Maybe her mom would realize that not working 24/7 wasn't such a bad thing and she'd find pleasure in something beyond work and shopping. Hey, if Mom lightened up because of dating Mr. Daniels, perhaps Robert would see that there's more to life than work and even he'd begin to chill. Then Sam could weasel more free time for herself. This would be a huge win-win for all involved.

It wasn't long before the kitchen was filled with the awesome smell of rich, delicious tomato sauce. As she stirred the sauce, Sam suddenly found herself feeling all warm inside; a little grin spread across her face.

Carlos, busy chopping onions, caught sight of this. "You having fun?"

Sam nodded and softly replied, "Yeah. We don't have the time to do this anymore. My mom's always too busy and we eat out way too often. This is reminding me of life before Danni became a star; we all used to work together to make dinner."

"I understand," he said, putting small handfuls of the minced veggies into the sauce. "I used to love helping my mom cook. She taught me how to get the best flavors out of different foods. When I do this now, I feel like she's still with me."

Sam was on the verge of telling Carlos how awesome she thought he was, but she couldn't find her voice. Instead of speaking, she looked him directly in the eye and offered a sympathetic smile. For the very first time, she didn't feel embarrassed or self-conscious doing this. In fact, she was surprised to discover that this quiet communication with him felt comfortable.

Carlos smiled back. The two of them stood there silently for a bit. It was really nice; it was easy and uncomplicated. The moment was shattered by the ringing of Sam's iPhone. She flinched before reaching into her pocket and answering it.

"Hello? Oh, hi, Seth." Suddenly off-the-charts uncomfortable, Sam turned away from Carlos. "No," she mumbled into the phone. "I haven't checked my e-mail in a while. No, Robert isn't here. Why?"

Carlos took the spoon out of Sam's hand and gave her a signal to go talk, while he took over the sauce. Even though she really wanted to hang up on Seth, she scurried out of the kitchen and into the dining room.

"Sorry, Seth. I couldn't hear. What'd you say?"

After sharing one seriously snarky sigh, Seth repeated himself, "There's a party at a new jewelry store this evening. I scored an invite. You in?"

"A party at a jewelry store?" Sam wasn't sure she understood. "That doesn't sound like fun. What would we do, eat nachos while wearing necklaces, try out tiaras as we test-taste tacos?" She giggled at her own silliness. "Binge on bling?"

Seth didn't laugh. "It's a major thing to be seen at

this party. There will be a ton of press and lots of important people. I thought you were committed to the success of our show, but hey – if you don't want to go with me – it's your call."

Sam wanted to tell Seth that being *committed to the success of their show* didn't mean she had to be dragged around to every public event like some prize-winning puppy, but she bit the insides of her cheeks to stop herself. Glancing around the dining room, she saw how much work still had to be done to make Operation Cupid the success it absolutely had to be, so all her energy went into trying to make Seth go away.

"I'm sorry, Seth, but there's no way I can go out tonight. We have some mega-important family stuff going on over here and I have to stay in."

There was a very long, strange silence.

"Uhh, Seth? You there?"

"Yeah, yeah, still here."

More silence.

"Uhh, Seth? Look I'm really truly sorry I can't go out with you tonight." Desperate to end the phone call, Sam blurted out, "How about tomorrow night? Could we make plans for tomorrow night?"

Immediately, the Seth Sam had come to know returned. "That'll work. I think there's a movie premiere I could get us invited too. I'll shoot you an e-mail as soon as I have it secured. You'd be in for a movie premiere, wouldn't you?"

Happy he couldn't see her rolling her eyes, Sam forced herself to sound positive. "Sure, Seth. See you tomorrow. Gotta go! Bye."

Sam hit the *end call* button as fast as she could and ran back into the kitchen.

"Get over here!" Olga demanded. "You *have* to taste this sauce! I knew my cuz was good, but I didn't know he was this good!"

Carlos held out a spoon. Sam expected something tasty, but was blown away by the flavor. "*Hello!*" she hollered as she licked her lips and put her hand on Carlos's shoulder. "Who knew we had our very own Jamie Oliver here?"

He smiled back and she suddenly realized she was touching him. Immediately embarrassed, Sam pulled back her hand and knocked over the basket of sliced bread on the counter. As fast as she could, she bent over to pick it all up without seeing Carlos doing the exact same thing. They clonked heads – hard. Sam landed on the ground while Carlos managed to stay standing. Both momentarily stunned, they looked at each other before bursting out laughing.

Olga pointed to the clock. "Very funny, Laurel and Hardy, but we don't have time for this."

Carlos, rubbing the rising bump on his head while helping Sam to her feet asked, "What did she call us?"

"Not what – *who*," Sam answered as she fought to get the giggles to go away. "They're old movie actors who did all kinds of slapsticky stuff. They were a great comedy team, you know, like Bert and Ernie from the Muppets."

As the words left her mouth, Sam cringed with regret. *Doofus!* she said to herself. *Carlos is going to think you're a big loser for watching kiddie videos – just like Seth did.*

For a second, Carlos stared blankly at Sam. She wished with all her might she could rewind that last stupid statement.

But then Carlos snapped his fingers. "Ah! You mean *Beto* and *Enrique*! The orange one with the rubber duck and the tall one with the banana head, yes?"

Sam nodded cautiously. Things with Carlos had been going so well. Why couldn't she have just zipped her lips and kept her quirky taste in videos as a private guilty pleasure?

"I love those guys!" Carlos exclaimed. "They were always my favorites."

That was it? No funny look? No snarky tone? Sam couldn't believe the big smile on Carlos's face. *He likes the Muppets*, she realized. *He doesn't think watching those videos is dumb or weird at all!*

"Seriously, you guys," Olga scolded them, "Mr. Daniels and Mrs. Devine will be here in about five minutes. Sam, go finish setting the table. Carlos, refill that bread basket. This is the final countdown, people. Move, move, move!"

Everyone raced around taking care of important details. Sam was just lighting the candles when she heard the front door open. She popped her head into the kitchen to say, "Someone's here," as she headed toward the hallway.

There she found Danni giving her mom a hug.

"Thanks for going with me, Mom," she said. "Sorry I can't stay for dinner but I promised Thomas we'd discuss his ideas for the backyard patio. I won't be out late."

Danni winked at Sam and stepped out the door just as Mr. Daniels walked up the steps.

"I'm here as promised," he said warmly. "Sam told me you wanted me here at seven-fifteen and according to my watch, it's seven-fifteen exactly."

Rose appeared confused. "I made no such request. In fact, I was out getting a manicure when I got an e-mail from Sam saying she needed my help with her homework and begged me to come home for an early dinner so she could get a good night's sleep before tomorrow's rehearsals."

The two adults slowly turned to face Sam.

She opened her arms wide. "How we all got here isn't important. Why don't we head into the dining room? Dinner is ready and waiting!"

Sam spun around and walked away quickly. She waited at the entrance of the dining room. Rose and Mr. Daniels followed. Sam loved the expressions on both their faces as they glanced around the dressed-up dining room. It was beautiful; there were gold candles all around and red rose petals covering the white tablecloth. Sam pulled out a chair for Rose and directed Mr. D to sit opposite her.

Olga slipped out of the kitchen and served two very carefully constructed salads.

"*Bueno appetito*," she said before whisking out of the room.

Sam turned to leave, but was stopped by her mom grabbing her arm and asking, "What is this all about?"

Clasping her hands in front of her, Sam simply explained, "Mom, tonight is all about you enjoying yourself. You've earned a quiet, candlelit dinner. And Mr. D," she gave him a nod, "you deserve a night off as well. Chill, have some wine, and let your master chef and outstanding waitstaff take care of you."

Backing out of the dining room and into the kitchen, Sam immediately pressed her ear against the door. It was silent for a while, but then she heard the sound of the cork popping as it came out of the wine bottle.

Olga, listening as well, got all excited. "They're opening the wine!" she whispered. "That's a really good sign!"

"Yeah," said Carlos, still stirring the sauce, "it's a good sign that they're thirsty. You two get away from there. If one of you serves the pasta and the other one stirs the sauce I can tune my guitar."

The girls did as they were told, but Sam couldn't stand not knowing what was happening in the room. She plopped the noodles on the plate as fast as she could so that she could run back to the door. Pushing it open ever-so-slightly, she heard her mom speaking.

"It's been such a long time since I've talked about anything other than business," Rose let out a gentle giggle, "that I can't think of anything else to discuss."

"What are they saying?" Olga hissed at Sam.

"They're talking about what to talk about," she answered.

Olga gave Sam a big thumbs up signal. "That's good! It means they're making an effort to communicate. That's important."

Sam giggled and quickly went back to listening.

"Sam is a great girl," Mr. Daniels said. "She mentions you all the time. Being a single parent couldn't have been easy, but you must know that you've done an amazing job."

"What are they saying now?" Olga hissed again.

"Mr. D complimented Mom on being a great mother."

"Yes!" Olga pulled her fist in to her hip, as if signaling a big victory. "That's excellent! Complimenting her mothering skills will make her feel appreciated and deserving of love. It'll also show her that he has a tender side."

Sam turned and folded her arms in front of her body. "Maybe Carlos was right about you watching too many sappy love movies."

Olga waved her hand at Sam. "Shhh! Go back to listening!"

Carlos came back into the kitchen with his guitar. "How's it going in there?"

"Olga has them running off to get married before we serve dessert," Sam replied with a sly grin.

Pretending to be all offended, Olga huffed, "*After* dessert," and stuck her tongue out at Sam.

Sam returned the gesture, but it was hard to keep her tongue sticking out while laughing. "Ow!" she cried.

Both Olga and Carlos shushed her.

"Sorry," she mumbled as she touched her hand to her tongue, "I think I just bit off a chunk."

"There's no blood gushing out," Carlos said as he carefully poured the sauce over the noodles. "You'll live long enough to serve my world-famous pasta à la Carlos."

Sam carefully pushed her back against the door and glided carefully into the dining room. Even though the lighting was low and the décor screamed romantic, Rose and Mr. Daniels were discussing how much time Sam had to spend memorizing her lines.

Rose reached out for Sam. "Little Bit, did you get the latest script changes? I got a text from the set that they were rewriting that final scene of episode one again."

Standing tall and speaking very properly, Sam admonished her mother. "Excuse me, but tonight, I am not *Little Bit*, I am Samantha, your server, and I'm hoping you will enjoy your main course and perhaps talk about something besides me or Danni or show business. Mr. Daniels, don't you think my mom looks lovely tonight? Mom? Don't you think the color of Mr. Daniels's tie complements his eyes?" She reached for the bottle of wine. "Would either of you like a little more vino?"

Both adults sat stone still. When she didn't get an

answer, Sam took it upon herself to go ahead and refill their wine glasses. She then set down the bottle and stealthily exited the dining room for the safe confines of the kitchen.

"Olga, I don't think this is working," she whispered to her friend.

"I have not yet begun to fight – for romance, that is!" Olga pushed Carlos toward the kitchen counter. "Carlos, romantic guitar music!"

"You both do know this is very cheesy, yes?" Carlos asked.

Olga waved her hand at him. "Less talk, more music – *now*!"

Hopping up onto the counter, Carlos opened the little shutters on the sliding partition between the kitchen and the dining room. He played his guitar and the beautiful music gently filled both rooms.

Leaning against the door to listen, Olga poked Sam, who was standing right next to her doing the exact same thing. "Why aren't they speaking?" she asked.

Sam shrugged and shook her head.

"Maybe they need some encouragement." Olga turned and snapped her fingers to get Carlos's attention.

"We need the smooching song," she demanded.

He abruptly stopped playing one tune and switched to another. The girls listened intently, but still, there was no discussion going on in the dining room.

Olga nudged Sam. "Ask me the question."

Sam hesitated. "You can't be serious. I thought that idea was a joke."

"Come on," Olga urged. "Ask it!"

Sighing with resignation, Sam took in a big breath and loudly called out, "Hey, Olga, that's a beautiful song. What's it called?"

In an equally loud voice, Olga replied, "The song is, *Besame Mucho*."

Again, Sam hesitated, but Olga elbowed her to keep going. "*Besame Mucho?* That sounds lovely but what does it mean?"

Giving Sam a big thumbs up for a job well done, Olga practically yelled back, "It's Spanish for *kiss me a lot*."

Both girls returned to listening at the door. After another long moment of silence, they heard Rose asking Mr. Daniels, "Did you put Sam up to this?"

Mr. Daniels laughed and threw his hands in the air.

"No! No! I was about to ask you the same thing."

Rose giggled before responding. "I'm beginning to get the picture here. Let me guess, the flowers I received, they weren't from you?"

Sam whipped her head around to Olga. "You sent my mom flowers?"

Olga nodded excitedly. "A stroke of genius, don't you think?"

"Flowers?" Mr. Daniels asked. "You got flowers? I got a chocolate apple."

Again, Sam looked to Olga who was grinning from ear to ear. "Yeah – I figured he deserved a little something too," she squeaked with pride.

"From a *secret admirer*," both adults said at the same time.

Rose's voice was full of good humor: "I should jinx you right now, but seeing as we're the only two here, it would get pretty lonely having no one else to talk to."

"Rose! *Rose!*" Robert's voice rang out so loud that it echoed.

"Oh no!" Sam winced. "What's he doing here?"

Olga grabbed Sam's arm. "I thought you said he was out of town for the day!"

"I guess he's back!" she cried. "He's going to ruin everything. How do I stop him?"

Carlos slipped down from the counter and stood next to Sam. "You don't," he said kindly. "This was a sweet thing to do for your mother, but you can't treat people like toys. Let the grown-ups deal with their own lives."

Robert stormed into the kitchen. "Sam, where is your mother? What's the point of her having a cell phone if she never answers it? I need her approval on several deals and can't..." He sniffed the air. "Something smells delicious. Am I too late for supper?"

Sam wanted to hush Robert and hustle him out of the house, but she glanced over at Carlos, nodded, and reached for a plate. As she did this, Rose called out from the dining room.

"Robert, I'm in the dining room chatting with Mr. Daniels. Come and join us."

Balancing a huge helping of pasta à la Carlos on one hand with his heavy briefcase in the other, Robert made his way into the dining room.

Olga, Sam and Carlos stood silent in the kitchen

until Sam disappointedly declared, "It's official. *Operation Cupid* has gone down in flames."

"Aw." Olga frowned. "Don't worry, Sam. I've got a few more tricks up my sleeve."

"No, Olga." Sam shook her head. "Tonight was a total hoot and a half, but we need to let it go. It's not fair to try to direct other people's personal lives. I guess since I've had so many people suddenly directing mine, I kind of forgot that."

The three friends ate their own massive servings of pasta and slowly got to work cleaning up the kitchen. About an hour later, Mr. Daniels brought his plate into the kitchen and set it in the sink.

"Thanks for the delicious dinner," he said as he rubbed his stomach. "I'm stuffed to the gills." He turned to Sam. "I'm honored that you think I'm good enough for your mom. She's an amazing woman and I truly enjoy spending time with her. If I weren't already seeing someone, I'd have asked her out on a date myself."

Sam's heart dropped to her knees. She hadn't thought to ask if Mr. Daniels already had someone special in his life. Not seeing him with a wedding ring, she'd assumed he was available.

Mr. Daniels headed toward the front door. "I can show myself out. Thanks again, kids."

Sam dropped her head forward and moaned slowly. "I am a *total* mo-mo."

Carlos laughed and put an arm around Sam's shoulders. "I don't know what a mo-mo is, but I'm sure you aren't one."

Oh! Sam was very aware of the feel of Carlos's arm on her shoulder. She slowly turned her head to look up at him, but the sudden ringing of the doorbell shattered the moment. Sam and Carlos both froze, but then the bell rang again and Carlos dropped his arm.

"Who would be *so rude* as to pop over at this time of night?" Sam growled loudly in frustration as she hurried over to find out for herself.

CHAPTER 12

Peeking through the eyehole, Sam was stunned to see Seth.

"What are you doing here?" she asked.

"Hey, Sammy-girl! I've got to talk to you."

Majorly annoyed, but strangely curious, Sam opened the door.

"Are you okay?" she asked. "Why are you here so late?"

Looking mighty pleased, Seth rocked back and forth on his feet while holding something behind his back. "It's not late," he said. "I just left that big jewelry party to bring you something."

Trying to stay friendly, Sam bit the inside of her cheek and started explaining, "Seth, this isn't a good time. I told you I had something going on here tonight."

"Yeah, yeah," he brushed off her concerns, "I know, but I figured you'd be so happy with what I got for you that I couldn't wait until tomorrow. Pick a hand."

"What?"

"Pick a hand," he insisted.

Sam needed Seth to leave. She didn't have any time or interest in playing his little game or in spending a single minute with him. Plus, the last thing she needed was for Carlos to see Seth and get the wrong idea – just when things were going so well.

"Left," she pointed. "Your left hand."

"Ah, but you pointed to my right." Seth was obviously enjoying this. "Try again and be more specific."

Gritting her teeth, Sam poked his right arm. "This one."

He held it out in front of him with nothing in his hand. "Nope. Try again."

Clenching her jaw even tighter, Sam slugged his

other arm. "How about *this* one then?"

"Ouch! Wow, heck of a punch there, Sammy-girl." Seth winced but forced a laugh. "Remind me to stay on your good side."

Way too late for that, she thought.

Seth slowly turned his left arm round and opened his hand to reveal a small blue box. "Ta-dah!"

Sam stared at the box.

"Go on," he urged, "open it."

She reached for it, pulled off the top, and looked inside. There was another box. A velvet one.

"Seth," she pleaded. "If this is a joke, I really don't have—"

"No, no," he cut her off with another laugh. "Although that would have been funny. We should have the writers put that into a show. Go on – I promise you'll like what's inside."

Sighing impatiently, she struggled to get the velvet box out of the blue one, then pulled back the velvet lid and was stunned to see a very sparkly ring.

"What is this?" she stammered.

Seth threw his head back and guffawed as if that was the funniest thing he'd ever heard. "Man, you really are a great comedian!" He imitated Sam: "What is this?"

Feeling her temper starting to rise, Sam swallowed hard before replying. "Seth, I know this is a ring, but I don't know why you'd give me a ring. It's not like we're—" She stopped herself. Did he think they were dating? Was this some kind of *going steady* ring? She found herself both confused and mortified.

"Relax," Seth said as he reached out and removed the ring. "They were giving away all kinds of cool jewelry at this party tonight. I saw this and thought how much cooler it is than that flower thing you always wear."

Flower thing? Was he talking about the beautiful silver rose ring? Sam loved that ring and hadn't taken it off, except to bathe, since Olga had given it to her last week. Seth grabbed Sam's hand to pull the rose ring off her finger.

"Excuse me?" she snapped as she pulled back her hand. "You *so* did not just grab my hand and try to take off my ring without asking my permission. I mean, a smart guy like you, you'd *totally* know better than to grab another person like that, right?"

Seth curled his lip and stared at her with a confused expression. He removed his baseball cap to scratch his head and fuss with his hair. Sam read all this fidgeting as Seth being super-uncomfortable, and under normal circumstances, she'd have made some effort to lighten the moment, but right then, she was so tweaked that she let him stand there, struggling to figure out what to do or say next. However, she was absolutely desperate to get back inside to Olga and Carlos.

"Seth," she said slowly, "I appreciate your wanting to give me something meaningful but—"

"Hang on!" Seth put both hands in front of his body. "This isn't some promise ring! We aren't a couple or anything! You didn't think…" He suddenly stopped speaking. An amused smile broke across his face. It was annoyingly clear he was about to start laughing again.

Sam's face burned a hot, embarrassed red. "No! No way! I didn't think we were…going out…dating… whatever." It didn't bother her that all the time she'd spent with Seth hadn't been for anything more than work, but the fact that he seemed so entertained by the very thought of her possibly thinking there was more to it – that was majorly mortifying.

Seth chuckled. "Here's the thing, Sammy-girl, people will notice you wearing that fancy ring and you can act shy and *reluctantly* admit that I gave it to you. This will get us even more publicity because everyone will think we are a real couple! You see how brilliant this is, don't you? Besides, that old flower thing you wear scratches me every time I grab your hand."

Sam toyed with the idea of throwing the fancy new ring right in the middle of Seth's annoying grin, but thinking about her mom stopped her. Rose was so proud of Sam for doing the show – something she thought Sam was doing because she really wanted it. This situation officially stunk like nasty old cheese. She remembered the poem Olga recited when she gave Sam the ring, *Friendship is like a shower of precious flowers*; Sam said a quick silent prayer that Olga would understand this mess. *Not wearing this ring for a week won't turn our friendship into a pile of weeds,* she thought, *will it?*

Sighing deeply, she officially made her decision, she'd only wear Seth's ring during rehearsals and when she was out with him. Any other time, she'd go right back to wearing Olga's beautiful silver rose.

"Okay," Sam said quietly as she slipped Olga's ring into her pocket and Seth's shiny one onto her finger. "I get it. Thank you."

Without even glancing up at him, she turned to head back into the house. "I've really got to get back in there. I'll see you at rehearsal tomorrow."

"Oh…about that."

Sam whipped back around to see Seth fiddling with his cell phone. It didn't seem as though he was actually reading anything, just making sure he didn't make eye contact with Sam.

"I picked up a three-day commercial shoot in Vancouver. I'll e-mail Mr. Victorio and tell him I've got the flu. That'll ensure he'll be more than happy with me missing a couple of days to recover as long as *you* don't make a fuss about it. I already know all my lines. I'm a total professional; this stuff comes naturally to me. You're the newbie. You need the rehearsal way more than I do. They can just have someone stand in for me and read you my lines. You'll be all right, yeah? You'll back me up on this, won't you, Sammy-girl?"

Sam bit her lip. Is this what she had to look forward to? Was working with Seth going to be all about managing his ego and covering his lies? She'd been so in awe of him the first time they'd met – he was wicked cute and seemed so cool and confident – but along with that, he was a first-class liar and a total rat. If it weren't for the stupid TV show, she'd have ripped him up one side and down the other, but that was the problem, the TV show. No Seth, no show, no staying in the mansion and no money to take care of Rose. Even though it shredded her insides, Sam gulped down the lump in her throat and nodded.

"That's my girl!" Seth gave her a half-hearted hug and hightailed it back to his limo.

As he opened the rear door he called out to her, "Remember to act worried about me. The more upset you seem about my *terrible sickness*, the better it will play in the gossip magazines."

Sam stepped inside, closed the door behind her, stared at it for a moment, and then kicked it so hard it sent a wave of pain up her entire spine. Wincing, she turned herself so she could lean against that very solid door and slid down to the floor. Carlos quietly appeared and slid down next to her.

"You are okay?" he asked.

She nodded, although her quivering lip was a pretty big giveaway that she wasn't.

There was a moment of silence before Carlos spoke again.

"Who was it?"

Barely able to speak without crying, Sam squeaked, "Seth."

"Did he upset you?"

Sam shook her head, but she didn't speak. Another quiet moment passed.

"Because," he said, "if he did, I'd be happy to talk to him, to explain that he made you unhappy, to stomp on the little cockroach."

That got Sam's full attention. Her head shot up and she turned to see Carlos smiling at her. Oh! He was trying to cheer her up. He was sitting so close to her that his shoulder was touching hers. He looked deep into her eyes and for a moment, Sam thought he was moving his head toward her. *Hey! He's going to kiss me,* she thought. *Whoa! I'm about to get that first kiss! Am I ready? Is this a perfect moment? I haven't thought this far ahead yet! Shouldn't I have been expecting this? I wasn't expecting this! What do I do?*

So excited she couldn't breathe, Sam began to babble. "No." She half laughed, half gasped for air and inadvertently pulled away just enough to kill the moment.

"Oh no, no no," she stammered while bashing the back of her head against the wall. "There's no need to stomp on him – at least, not yet." Mad at herself for opening her big dumb mouth and breaking the flow of what could have been her first kiss, she absent-mindedly held up the hand with the new ring on it. It felt so wrong on her hand. She missed the lovely solidness and weight of Olga's flower ring; this shiny thing felt thin and flimsy.

"That's new," Carlos commented.

"It's not what you think!" Sam got flustered. She didn't want Carlos to get the wrong impression. "It's for work. Seth wants the paparazzi to think we are going out so they'll put our pictures in their magazines and hopefully that will get more people to watch our TV show."

"That sounds…" Carlos seemed to have to think for the right word, "dishonest."

Sam cringed. She wanted to argue that it wasn't dishonest, it was more like a game, a joke – but she couldn't. "Yeah," she nodded slowly. "It is pretty dishonest."

Carlos looked directly at Sam. "Being dishonest is hardly *pretty*."

"I didn't mean it that way." She waved her hands. "Being dishonest is so *not* pretty. I wasn't saying, that is…I was trying to explain that—"

"You were trying to say that what you and little cockroach are doing is only a *little* dishonest." Carlos's tone got more serious. "I understand. I just don't think there is such a thing as being a *little* dishonest. Either you are honest or you are not."

Sam gritted her teeth. This discussion was not going well. "It's not a big thing. This isn't something major; it's more like a little white lie."

"Yes," Carlos nodded, "a lie."

"Hang on," Sam shook her head to try and clear it. "I didn't mean a *lie* lie; it's not as if the point was to fool or trick…"

She bit her lip. The point *was* to let people think that she and Seth were an item and that was not true. Carlos was dead right; what she was doing with Seth was dishonest.

"Are you going to wear that ring then?" Carlos asked.

Sam pulled it off her finger and put it in her pocket. "I don't know. It's complicated."

Carlos stood up. He held out his hand to Sam. She grabbed it and stood up next to him. He looked her square in the eye.

"No," he said. "It's not complicated. You only need to make a decision. You know wearing it is dishonest. Do you want to be honest or not?"

Click click click, clack clack click.

I am the BIGGEST DOOFUS on the face of the earth!!! Tonight, I *almost* got my first kiss! And from a guy I like so much he makes my toes curl. *ALMOST!* I had the perfect opportunity to tell… wait…let's call my special guy *Mr. C* (as if I'm dumb enough to put his real name online). Anyway, I had the perfect moment to tell *Mr. C* that I like him – *like him* like him – and I chickened out. But it wasn't a total chicken out, because – aargh, this is soooo complicated!

Mr. C seems like he's about to kiss me and I panic and chatter away — totally killing the moment. <u>*URGH!!!*</u> I have a friend who told me to chill out and "enjoy being a goofy teenager," but I'm not enjoying much of anything right now.

This is beyond unfair! It truly was *the* perfect moment, there was no drama, no trauma, no shenanigans. None of that fake, set-up stuff you see on TV or in the movies. There will *never* be such a totally perfect moment for a first kiss again.

Sam hit the "send" button. Even once the post was live on her blog, she just sat in her chair. Too much had gone on in one night. She'd loved her time with Olga and that private chat with Carlos had been painfully delicious, but the intrusion by Seth had only reminded her how *complicated* everything felt nowadays. Was she totally wrong thinking Carlos *liked her* liked her? What was up with Seth giving her that ring? He'd made it very clear that he *didn't like her* like her, so why was it so important to him that everyone else should think he *liked her* liked her? Why *didn't* he *like her* like her?

Sam gently tapped on the hidden microphone by her computer. "Blu?" she asked gently. "Are you there? I need to ask you a question."

There was no response.

This is what life is like now with him working on the stables show instead of The Devine Life, she thought sadly as she reached her hand around to grab a hidden can of orange cream soda, only to find that there wasn't one.

Determined to make one thing go her way this rotten night, Sam decided to sneak downstairs and snag a can from the pantry, but as she slipped out her bedroom, she noticed the light on in Danni's room.

She tapped gently on the door and asked in a hushed tone, "Danni? You awake?"

The door flew open so fast it frightened Sam enough to get her to jump back.

Danni stood in the doorway with an expression of pure astonishment. "Did my little sister just knock before entering my bedroom?" she asked dramatically.

"Yeah, yeah," Sam looked down at her feet. "I know I've been horrible about that. But—" She was beyond embarrassed about the question she wanted to ask. "See, I need someone to be *totally* honest with me. *Please* don't laugh at me, but...but..."

"But..." Danni asked breathlessly, "but *what*?"

"Okay..." Sam put her hands over her eyes, "do you think I'm pretty enough to have a boyfriend?"

Danni grabbed Sam's hands and marched her over to the bed where she pushed her down into a sitting position, sat next to her, and looked directly into Sam's green eyes.

"You listen to me, Little Bit," Danni ordered. "Asking if you are *pretty enough to have a boyfriend* is the *dumbest* thing I've ever heard come out of your mouth."

Sam pulled away from her sister. Danni's harsh words felt like a punch in the gut.

"Let's be clear," Danni continued. "I'm not saying *you* are dumb or you having a crush is dumb. It's thinking that the whole having a boy- or girlfriend is based on *how you look* that is *hardcore stupid*. Having someone special in your life is wicked cool as long as it's for the *right reasons*. You want to pick a guy who likes you for *you*; for who you are, not for how you look. And it goes both ways. Don't decide some dude should be your boyfriend just because you think he's *cute* or *dreamy*." Danni pretended to throw-up. "Ask yourself, is this guy a nice person? Can you talk to him? Does he get your humor? You want a boyfriend who is first and foremost your friend – a real friend, someone you can trust. Get me?"

"Yeah, I guess so," Sam replied. This was what Olga had talked about – being Carlos's friend as well as his girlfriend. How come everybody knew this stuff except for Sam? She sighed before glancing over and realizing that Danni wasn't too happy with her wimpy response, so she threw her arms out wide. "Yes! Yes! I understand. I really do! I hear exactly what you're saying."

Danni seemed rather pleased with herself. "Look at me, giving good advice to my little sister." She reached her arms around and patted herself on the back.

Sam loved seeing Danni all happy and nutty again. The real Danni Devine was back!

"And now, Miss Thing, that's enough wisdom for

one night. March back to your room and hit the hay," Danni ordered authoritatively.

Sam saluted her sister. "Sir, yes sir! I hear and obey." She ran out of the room and did a flying leap into her own bed.

CHAPTER 13

The next morning, Sam, still wearing her clothes from the previous evening, was lying in bed wide awake long before her alarm buzzed at 5:30. She'd been replaying her uncomfortable moments with both Seth and Carlos over and over in her head and trying to tie it all together with all the advice she'd had recently from Olga, Blu, and Danni. Mom and Robert had made it clear that they were friends who could work together; Sam should be able to do the same with Seth, right? Lost in her own thoughts, the buzzing at exactly 5:30 surprised her so much she almost fell out of bed.

As she sat up to reach over and shut off the alarm,

Rose burst into the room, startling Sam so much that she actually did end up tumbling out of her bed onto the floor.

"Sam!" Rose cried out at the top of her lungs as she kneeled down to help her daughter. "I'm so sorry! I was waiting until your alarm went off before I came in to tell you the exciting news. Are you all right?"

"I'm fine, Mom," Sam yelled over the buzzer, "but can you shut off that awful alarm?"

Rose reached up and tried hitting every button, but the alarm continued. In frustration, she yanked on the cord and pulled it out from the wall. The noise ended abruptly.

Both Devines needed a couple of moments to gather themselves in the blissful silence, but it didn't last very long. Suddenly Robert's voice rang out from the hallway and filled Sam's room.

"Is she up yet? Is she dressed? The plane leaves in one hour and we've got to be sure she knows her lines."

"One minute, Robert," Rose answered back. She turned her attention to Sam and helped her to her feet. "Sweetie, there's a big kids' award show tonight in New

York City and Seth was supposed to present an award, but the poor boy is sick with the flu, so you need to fill in for him. Come on – take a quick shower and throw on some jeans and a T-shirt. Robert's chartered a private plane so we can all go. Even Jean and Jehan are flying with us so they can get you ready on the flight. You have a little routine to memorize, some speech you need to give as you present the award. Isn't this exciting? Come on – let's go!"

With no time to think, Sam was pushed out into the hallway and down to her bathroom. She took a super-fast shower, which wasn't hard to do with Rose outside the door yelling at her to hurry up. Before she was aware of what was going on, she was in the limo, holding an apple in one hand and a script in the other.

The flight to New York should have been fun. Flying in private jets usually is. But this trip was all about pressure. The little speech Sam had to learn was lame; the *big* punchline of the *big* joke was so not funny that Sam cringed every time she read it. Jean and Jehan took turns torturing her, whether it was flat-ironing her hair with the setting on super-hot so it practically fried her ears off or sticking her with safety pins in an effort to make some silly sequined outfit look as if it actually fit her. As the plane got close to New York and Sam finally felt she'd memorized her little speech, a fax printed out with an entirely different speech and the news that they'd changed the award they wanted Sam to give so she'd get better family exposure. None of this made any sense to Sam, all she could do was listen to the instructions being barked at her and try not to freak out – even though it was pretty clear that every adult around her was worried – this whole awards thing was obviously rather important.

What made it even worse was getting an e-mail from Mr. Daniels upon landing, asking where she was. When Sam asked her mom why nobody had mentioned the trip to him, Rose got all flustered and blamed Robert, who made some cheeseball excuse and said, "She's only missing one day of school, it's no big deal."

That set Rose off *big time*. The entire limo ride to the award ceremony, Rose and Robert argued, Jean and Jehan continued to primp Sam and at the same time she was *still* trying to learn her lines. The limo pulled up in front of a huge theater with a massive red carpet and paparazzi flashing their cameras all over the place.

One of the twins strapped a pair of rather tall wedge-heeled sandals on to Sam's feet and warned her, "Walk slowly, zees are a leetle beeg for you," before pushing her out of the door.

There she stood, on some enormous red carpet, with all the chaos and commotion of the world focusing on her, and when she went to take her first step, her *leetle too beeg* sandals almost caused her to trip and fall. Trying to smile, she slowly shuffled along the carpet, waving to the crowd as they yelled her name and shouted for an autograph. It was the most horrifying moment of her life. By the time she actually stepped inside the theater, Rose and Robert had rushed around the crowd and were waiting to half-guide, half-carry Sam to the backstage part of the theater.

Finally getting a moment to look around, Sam peered out from behind the curtain and saw that the theater was full of kids and there didn't appear to be an empty seat.

"You're giving the first award of the evening," Rose

explained as she patted Sam on the back. "Don't be nervous. Just smile and say your lines, then open the envelope and read the name of the winner. You can do this."

Sam tried to nod, but instead of her head going up and down, it felt as if her entire body was shaking. The lights in the theater flashed twice before going down. An orchestra began playing, and an announcer's voice boomed out so loudly it hurt Sam's ears.

"Welcome, everyone," the voice shouted, "to the third annual Kids Count Awards show! Here to present the first award of the evening, the star of this fall's most anticipated new series, *Stable Stories*, and everyone's favorite little sister, Sam Devine!"

The roar of the crowd made Sam want to turn and run, but Robert pushed her toward the stage. Practically falling off her sandals, Sam forced a grin and carefully made her way to the center of the stage where a single spotlight was waiting for her. As she reached the spot, the light blinded her and she ended up hitting the microphone with her nose. That made the audience giggle. Swallowing hard, Sam somehow managed to remember her lines and say them perfectly, although, the new speech had an even unfunnier joke in it with an even stinkier punchline which didn't get a single laugh. Mortified at the silence, she read the names on the front of the envelope, but when she tried to turn it around to open it, it slipped through her fingers. She bent down to pick it up and rammed her head into the mike stand, hard. The audience gasped. Desperate to get through the moment, Sam grabbed the envelope and stood back up, but as she tried to stand, she slipped off her sandal and fell flat on the ground. The audience, thinking it had to be an act, began to laugh. Beyond mortified, Sam again tried to stand once more, but the hem of her dress was under her other sandal, so as she stood, a terrible ripping sound rang out and was heard by the entire audience. This made everyone laugh even harder. When she finally got to a standing position and tore open the envelope, her hands were shaking so hard that she bumped the microphone again and the paper inside the envelope flew out and landed on the ground. This made the audience howl. Not wanting to continue making a complete fool of herself, Sam pulled the mike off its stand and sat on the ground. She grabbed the paper and read the name of the winner. The audience applauded wildly and a tall young man raced up from the audience to accept his award. As he gave his acceptance speech, Sam stayed on her spot, on the ground, unable to move. The young man finished his thank-you speech and then bent down, picked Sam up, and carried her offstage. The roar of laughter and applause from the audience was deafening.

Once they got backstage, the young man set Sam down and shook her hand.

"That was awesome!" he crowed. "You are hilarious! We'll be on every entertainment show around the world tonight! Thank you for that! You made me look like a hero!"

Before Sam could answer, Robert and Rose appeared and whisked her away to a quiet spot in a corner of the backstage area.

Robert was smiling so hard, Sam thought his glorious white teeth might fall right out of his head. "Brilliant! That was positively genius! You just got us the best publicity money could buy. Samantha, I was worried you couldn't pull this off, but wow – you really are a natural!"

Yeah, Sam thought, *a natural disaster!*

Rose hugged Sam so hard it knocked all the wind out of her lungs. "Oh, Little Bit, I'm so proud of you! That was the funniest thing I've ever seen! You really are a born comedian."

Sam didn't have the heart to tell them that what they had just witnessed was no act; it was just her nerves making her even more of a klutz than she usually was. Unable to speak for fear she'd burst into tears, Sam grimaced, shook her head and waved her hands as if to say, "It was nothing."

Robert looked at Rose. "Would you like to stay and make an appearance at the after-show party?"

"NO!" Sam interjected forcefully.

When both adults stared down at her with expressions that made it clear she'd stunned them, Sam tried to cover her tracks. "I mean, I'm so exhausted. I need to get home because tomorrow I'll have double the schoolwork to do along with all my lines, so no thank you, no more show, no party, let's go home."

Click click click, clack clack click.

Hello Faithful Blog Readers,

Being a righteous klutz, I managed to totally, utterly, & 100 percently humiliate myself on national television tonight.

How was your Monday? (deep sigh)

The irony is that *everyone* thought I *planned* my "routine" and now there's press out there calling me the "most promising young comedian in recent memory"! HUH??

Showbiz is the *dumbest* biz EVER!

I have to go to bed now. The rest of this week is going to be a treadmill of terror with more rehearsals and more fittings and more interviews and more tutoring and...(you get the ugly picture).

I'd say, *more soon* — but I don't know if I'll ever have another moment to myself to blog again. If I don't, just know I love blogging and I'll miss you — my readers (that means you, Olga).

(DEEEEEEEEEEEEEEEEP SIGH)

Click click click, clack clack click.

Hey, look at this, only twenty-four hours after my last blog and I have managed to steal away a little time to write to you. Today was all rehearsal, rehearsal, rehearsal.

Imagine having to do the same thing over and over again — but each time tweaking one tiny element, like where you should put your left foot when you say one particular word or exactly how you need to turn your head to get a clean profile (what does that mean? My nose is my nose — how can it look so different from one camera angle to another???) and still you have to be absolutely perfect or they make you start all over again. It's insane.

And with Seth sick (not going to comment on this except to say — grrrrrrrr), they have a stand-in taking his place. So there I am, trying to act

(I should say trying to LEARN how to act) with some poor stagehand who got stuck reading Seth's lines off the page (and doing so with as much enthusiasm as cold, wet spaghetti).

Man-oh-man, I just re-read what I've typed here and YIKES — I sound downright snarky. That's not cool, but I realize it and am going to deal with it head on.

Tomorrow will be a better day. Tomorrow will be a better day. Tomorrow will be a better day. (If I say it/type it enough times, it comes true, right?)

8-)

Click click click, clack clack click.

Yesterday I blogged that today (yesterday's tomorrow) would be a better day. WRONG!! Today was even worse! They made me run those same scenes as yesterday, but each time in a different outfit. And of course, the one pair of pants that were *truly uncomfortable* (they ride up at the back so much they give me a total wedgie) are the ones that got picked as *my main outfit* — the thing I'll wear whenever my character is working at the stables (which is basically EVERY SINGLE SECOND OF THE SHOW). I hoped that maybe it was just this one odd pair that felt so wrong, but no, once they made the decision they brought out a whole rack of pants that were exactly the same. I tried on all twelve pairs and each one was just as bad as the first. (sigh)

Tomorrow they are going to decide on my riding hat. Yeah — can you think of anything more exciting than spending hour upon hour underneath egg-frying hot lights trying on hat after hat after hat after hat after... (deep sigh)

I knew doing a TV show wasn't going to be all fun and games but come on, how about a *little fun* already??? And seriously — doesn't anybody working on a TV show have any friends they'd like to see? I haven't had two minutes to see Olga. Every text I send is little more than another reason why we can't hang out. I've had to cancel on her three times already this week. I know she's getting annoyed with me — but what can I do?

Click click click, clack clack click.

Last night I blogged that today, Thursday, was going to be all about finding the right riding hat for me — well that was only *half* of the story. The rest of the day was about boots. I tried on loads and loads of boots and — *of course* — the ones *I* actually liked didn't "show well" on camera (huh?) so they picked the ugliest pair of hot pink cowboy boots ever made.

I spent my entire day (when I wasn't in the school trailer doing extra work to make up for missing Monday's lessons — Mr. Daniels is a great teacher, but man, he pours on the assignments!) running back and forth from the wardrobe to the set for costume and lighting checks. Honestly, for a girl who isn't going to school, I bet I've done more laps than anyone on any track team anywhere in the world!

Tomorrow is Friday and we begin shooting on Monday, so I'm prepared for one more awful day and then I get to hang out with Olga on Saturday and Sunday!! 8-)

By then things will have gelled and mellowed, right? RIGHT?!?!?!?

Click click click, clack clack click.

It's *SATURDAY.* I am blogging from the *set.* WHY am I blogging from the set on a SATURDAY when I should be out horseback riding with my best friend?

I have three minutes to tell you before my next interview. This will be the fourth out of the ten interviews I have...I mean *GET* – the fourth out of the ten interviews I *GET* to do today (see – I'm still staying positive – it'll pay off and things will get better…soon…*please*!!).

Every single interview is exactly the same:

- they have me sit on a bale of hay and tell me to look directly into the camera.
- then they stick an earpiece so far into my head that I worry it might pop out my nose.
- then they pin a tiny microphone on me, and warn that I cannot move because it's very sensitive and will pick up the rustling of my clothing and we'll have to start the interview all over again.
- AND THEN they remind me to smile and act as if I'm having the best time EVER.
- in-between each interview I get exactly four minutes to have my makeup touched up and (get ready to laugh) *rest*. LOL!

I must look like a complete doofus answering these questions that get piped directly into my brain. I have no idea who is actually interviewing me. I never get to see a face. For all I know, I could be speaking to aliens!

Okay, it's not *as* painful as I'm making it sound. *Here's* why I'm such a crankpot: Mom promised that I wouldn't have to work at all tomorrow, so I swore to Olga that we could ride from morning till night. But two minutes ago Mom told me that I need to stay at home and rest since Monday is our first shooting day. URGH!!!!

How insane is it to live in the same town as your best friend and NEVER get to see her?!?!?! I know this latest cancellation is really going to make Olga mad, but what can I do? Being this busy stinks like an eight-week-old egg salad sandwich (gag).

PS Just texted Olga about having to bail on tomorrow's plans and her answer was not good. She replied:

IT FIGURES.

That's all she wrote. I texted her back and begged her to come to the set on Monday (her dad *is* our producer – he'll be cool about her missing one day of school), but I wouldn't blame her if she didn't show up.

Please, Olga – if you are reading this – I am SO SORRY! I really MISS YOU! Please come to the set on Monday!! Please!!! *PLEASE?!?!?!*

CHAPTER 14

Sam lay still in her bed. She hadn't slept a wink. Here it was, the first day of shooting for her TV show and the pit in her stomach that appeared when she had climbed into bed the previous night had gotten progressively bigger with each tick of the clock on her nightstand. She had survived her mega-nasty week of rehearsals, fittings, interviews and other TV-show related insanity. It all lead up to *this* day.

"Rise and shine!" Rose called out as she entered Sam's room with a flourish. "I've brought breakfast in bed for my little TV star!"

Forcing a smile, Sam sat up. "Thanks, Mom. It smells great."

Rose set the tray on her daughter's bed and laughed. "Cornflakes and milk smell great? I must be a better chef than I thought! Eat up, Little Bit. We need to be out the door in exactly one hour. They are shooting all the outdoor scenes early so that there is plenty of time to set everything up for Danni's concert in that lovely outdoor arena." Rose continued chattering away as she straightened up the messy room. "When the director says you're done, rush back to your trailer and get cleaned up. Your sister has been rehearsing day and night to make this farewell concert her best one ever. I'm still not happy with Danni's decision to give up performing, but I have to admit I am so proud of how hard she's worked to make sure she leaves this chapter of her life on a positive note. She wrote lovely thank-you notes to all the crew from her past concerts and *The Devine Life*. That's the mark of a true professional, showing personal gratitude to everyone who supports you. Just like Seth's behaved this past week."

"*What?*" Sam almost knocked the tray off the bed.

"I am so impressed by how that young man has

called in every day to let each one of us – myself, Robert, Caesar and your director, Blu – know how he's doing," Rose explained as she tidied up. "Poor thing. Imagine, having the flu through the last week of rehearsals. It must have been awful for him."

Sam had to bite the insides of her cheeks not to scream. Seth – *the rat* – his three-day shoot in Vancouver had turned into an entire week! He'd texted her over and over, begging her to keep covering for him while he finished working on the commercial. Meanwhile he was calling Mr. Victorio and everyone else on the production team every day to moan about how sick he was. He'd lied to *everybody* and there was Rose thinking the little twerp was such a great guy.

While Sam fumed, Rose picked up a pair of jeans from the floor. "Oops," she said as she knelt down and scooped up the silver rose ring from Olga and the shiny one from Seth. She examined them for a moment before holding them out and asking, "I know one ring is from Olga, but where'd you get this other one, Sam?"

Sam leaped out of bed and grabbed the jewelry. "It's a long story, Mom," she said as she set the rings on her desk and headed out of her room. "I'll explain later."

Reaching the bathroom, she locked the door. She already had enough on her mind without needing to explain about Seth giving her a ring that truly meant nothing.

"Okay, honey," Rose called out. "See you downstairs."

After racing to get dressed, Sam tapped on her bedroom mirror. She really needed to speak to Blu. It was only morning, and already this day was feeling like more than she could handle. She tapped again, but there was still no answer. "Come on, Blu," she whined. She stepped over to her computer and leaned down to speak into a hidden microphone, but it wasn't there! Suddenly, Sam was overwhelmed; of course! Blu had gone! Michi was now the director of *The Devine Life*. She must have decided she didn't want the microphone in that spot and had it changed on Saturday while Sam was doing all those satellite interviews. With Danni's final concert tonight, the move to her new home tomorrow, and Sam's friendship with Blu limited to occasional chats on set, the life she'd lived for the past two years was really over.

Sam felt small and alone. Having Blu on the set of the new show wasn't anywhere near the same as knowing that he was only a tap on a hidden microphone away. The enormity of this hadn't hit her until now. She climbed under her desk and let hot stinging tears roll down her cheeks.

"Sam!" Rose's voice shot over the intercom.

"Yikes! Ouch!" Sam was so startled that she sat up straight and clonked her head.

"Samantha!" Rose screeched even louder.

Scrambling out from under the desk, she stretched to push the "talk" button.

"Yes, Mom?"

"Time to go, honey! You don't want to be late for your first day of filming!"

Drawing up all the energy she could, Sam answered, "You're right, Mom! No worries. Last one to the front door is a rotten egg!"

Sam was about to run out of the room, when she remembered the rings. She grabbed both, shoved them into her back pocket, and hurried out.

When the Devine family limo arrived at the stables, Sam looked around for Olga. Even though she tried to tell herself not to be upset – maybe Mrs. V wouldn't let Olga miss a day of school to visit Sam – not seeing her there made Sam feel even more alone.

And there was no sign of Carlos either. Not that she'd expected him or anything. They hadn't spoken at all since the *Operation Cupid* evening. Still, she couldn't help but hope that he'd make *some* effort to see her.

Jean and Jehan appeared and pounced on Sam. They babbled away in their fabulous Franglais as they worked their wardrobe, hair and makeup magic. Two hours later, Sam was released from their grip and walked toward the mirror on the trailer door, where she finally got to look at herself. Sam was stunned; she looked like a mini, brunette Danni!

"So?" Jean (or maybe it was Jehan) asked. "What do you zeenk?"

Sam had to translate. "What do I *think*? Well, I think I don't look like me."

The twin brothers squealed in delight. Sam hadn't really meant that as a compliment, but the guys were super pleased with the comment, so she didn't say anymore.

As she stepped out of the wardrobe trailer, the sun

hit her eyes. Momentarily blinded, she decided simply to sit on the trailer's steps rather than risk falling down them.

This was it. She was dressed, made-up, and expecting to take her place on the set. All the time and work of the past couple of weeks had lead up to this; the pressure was bone crushing. For a moment she thought she was going to throw up, then she worried she might cry, but remembering the heaps of mascara on her eyelashes and fearing tears would glue her eyelids shut, she lifted her hands to fan her pooling eyes. To her great surprise, someone grabbed her hands and lifted her to her feet.

"You okay?" a friendly voice asked.

"Carlos!" Sam gasped with delight. "You came!"

"We've been here for about an hour," Olga said. "Dad let us bail on school today. He figured you could use the *moral support.*"

Now Sam seriously *was* on the verge of crying — with relief. "You're here!" She leaped off the steps and hugged her best friend. "Olga, I've missed you! I haven't been avoiding you! I swear!"

Olga nodded. "Dad set me straight. I was grumping

around the house, feeling all abandoned, and he made it *very* clear to me that it was because of the show that you were too busy for me. I'm sorry I was such a bonehead."

"No apology necessary," Sam replied. "It's done. It's over. It's all good."

"Sam! Hey, Sam!" A young girl's shrill squeal pierced Sam's eardrum.

Sam's eyes got huge. "No!"

Olga nodded sadly. "Yes. Inga is *in love* with Seth. It's beyond pathetic."

Inga ran over and squeezed herself in between Sam and Carlos. "Are you excited? That's a silly question, I mean, how could you *not* be? Seth Black! You get to work with Seth Black! Is he not the hottest boy ever? Is this not the greatest day of your entire life? Could you not just eat that guy up with a spoon?"

Seth suddenly appeared from the other side of the trailer. "Sammy-girl!" He put an arm around Sam. "Did ya miss me?"

"Seth! It's you! Hi! Hi, Seth!" Inga squealed.

He barely acknowledged her existence. "Yeah."

Stepping closer, Inga held up a pink cardboard sign

with Seth's name printed on it in sequins. "Me and my fellow fashion club members made this for you! See," she pointed to a corner, "we all signed it, but my signature is the biggest because I'm the president of the fashion club! We all love you, but I love you the most! I'm going to hold this up while you shoot your scene!"

Making it clear that he wasn't interested, Seth sighed and made a show out of removing his arm from Sam's shoulder and then pulling a pen out of his pocket.

"Let me autograph your sign for you. What's your name, young lady?"

"Inga," she replied breathlessly, "Inga Victorio."

"V...Victorio?" Seth stammered.

Inga nodded with all her might.

Seth's entire demeanor changed. He stood straighter and focused his million-dollar grin on her. "Are you related to my friend Olga here?"

Shooting a displeased glance in her sister's direction, Inga's voice dropped from high-pitched happy to low and annoyed. "She's my sister."

Olga laughed. "Try not to sound so thrilled about that, Inga."

Ignoring Olga, Seth kept his focus on Inga while

autographing her sign. "It's very nice to meet you, Inga. Say, did your dad happen to mention anything about me missing all those rehearsals?"

Inga opened her mouth to answer, but Olga cut her off. "He didn't say much about you, Seth," she explained dryly. "He was busy making sure everything was ready for today – you know, doing his job. You should try it some time."

"Olga!" Inga frowned before turning back to Seth with adoration in her eyes. "You'll have to excuse my sister. She's not like us. She's not used to dealing with fabulous people – because Sam here is pretty much her only friend."

Sam raised her hand and proudly proclaimed, "Yup, that's me. Olga's one and only!"

Seth noticed Sam's hand. "Yo, Sammy-girl, where's my ring?"

"You gave a ring…to Sam?" Inga asked Seth with horror in her voice.

"I…I…it's in my pocket, Seth," Sam struggled. She hadn't discussed the ring situation with Olga and the last thing she could afford to do right now was upset her best friend when she needed her most. "*Along* with my silver flower from Olga. I don't think I'm allowed to wear any jewelry on the show."

"You gave a ring...to *Sam*?" a distraught Inga asked again.

"Seriously, Seth," Olga snorted. "You should know that a performer can't wear anything personal while they are working."

Seth seemed stunned for a second, but then he leaned toward Olga and snarled, "Just you watch," before walking away with attitude.

"You gave a *ring* to *Sam*?" Inga whined as she chased after him.

Sam let out a massive exhale. "Thank you for being so cool, Olga. I'm super-sorry I had to take off the silver rose. I've worn it day and night since you gave it to me."

"It's okay," Olga replied. "Carlos had already clued me in that *Twerpy* had given you one for another of his famous PR stunts. Come on, you think I'm so shallow I'd worry we weren't best friends still just because you had to take the ring off?"

Carlos had talked to Olga about the ring? He understood! He totally understood about Seth!

Someone tapped Sam on her left shoulder. When she looked and saw no one there, she thought it was Seth, back from his tantrum. She whipped around to her right, prepared to let him really have it. Instead, she found Blu and was so thrilled to see him she gave him a huge hug, almost knocking him down.

"Hey there," Blu said softly, "I'm happy to see you too, but remember, here, I'm your director – not your buddy." But he did hug her back.

Sam stood on her tiptoes and whispered, "I can't believe you're out of the house. It's so empty without you."

Blu's eyes got the tiniest bit watery, but he stepped back, cleared his throat and asked loudly, "Aren't you going to introduce me to your friends?"

Even though Blu knew so much about Sam and her world, he'd never met any of her friends. Sam had kept her promise and never told anyone about her friendship with him – not even Olga.

"Olga Victorio, Carlos Victorio, this is our director, Blu. His real name is—"

"Blu is fine," Blu cut her off with a laugh as he reached out and shook Carlos's hand. "It's nice to meet you, Carlos. And Miss Victorio." Blu shook Olga's hand politely. "I'm having a wonderful time working with your father. He is a genuinely good guy."

Blu's kind words about her dad made Olga light up like a Christmas tree.

Turning back to Sam, Blu tapped his watch. "Time on a set is very expensive, so let's not waste it. Go to position for this scene, please."

Sam deflated. With her mouth as dry as a desert, she nodded and took a couple of slow, cautious steps toward the set.

"Sam?" Olga called out.

Turning back slowly, Sam answered hesitatingly, "Yeah?"

Olga gave her friend the biggest thumbs up and the widest smile ever.

That made Sam feel a little better.

"And don't forget..." Carlos said, walking up to her. Once he was at her side, he leaned toward her.

Sam's heart stopped beating. *This is it! He's going to give me a good luck kiss*, she thought with a mix of fear and excitement. *Don't pull away! Stay calm. Here it comes — my first kiss!*

Instead, he whispered in her ear, "It's not easy being green."

What? Oh! That's a Kermit the Frog song! Carlos was trying to help her relax! She gave him a friendly slug in the arm before heading off.

As she got close to her mark, Sam was surprised to see Seth arguing with Mr. Victorio. She wanted to hear the conversation, but was stopped by a production assistant who made her hold still so she could put a tiny microphone pack on her. She duct-taped it to the small of Sam's back, then ran a wire up her shirt and taped the eeny-beanyiest microphone Sam had ever seen to the back of her neck.

"Is it supposed to be this uncomfortable?" Sam asked.

The production assistant laughed knowingly. "If you think it's bad now, wait until you go to pull it off." Then she gave Sam a friendly pat on the top of her head and said, "Break a leg," before walking over to join the rest of the crew. There must have been fifty people standing behind the line of tape on the ground that marked off the set from the work area! Blu was in front giving directions to everyone, but he definitely had one eye on the argument between Seth and Mr. Victorio.

"Young man," Mr. V said sternly, "as I've said *three times now*, I appreciate your efforts to drum up publicity for the show, but I do not think it's appropriate for a girl *my own daughter's age* to be wearing some ring a boy has given her."

"Do you believe that guy?" Seth grumbled as Mr. V walked away and Sam took her place next to him. "He should be thanking me for my brilliant idea and instead he shoots me down. What a loser."

"You *so* did not call my best friend's dad a loser," Sam snapped without thinking.

Seth waved her off. "Chill out, Sammy-girl. I can't help it if I'm the only forward-thinking person here. Did you hear our *big-time* director's latest decision?"

Sam was so stunned to hear anyone ever say anything negative about Blu that all she could do was shake her head.

"Instead of standing *next* to our horses, he wants us *on* them! How dumb is that?"

Sam cocked her head to the side. "Why is that dumb?"

Seth looked away. "It just is."

"Seth," Sam replied matter-of-factly, "you can't call a decision *dumb* for no reason. Blu is totally cool. If you have a *reason* why we shouldn't be on our horses, tell him. He'll listen."

Glaring at her, Seth snarked, "Well, look at you, *Miss I'm-Such-Good-Buds-With-The-Director*. I don't have to explain myself to you. I don't have to explain myself to anyone. It's a dumb idea because I say it is."

"Oh yeah," Sam shot back, "that's mature. I don't think it's dumb at all! I can't wait to get on my horse."

"Wait!" Seth stepped super-close and whispered in Sam's ear. "Listen, if you *have* become such good friends with Blu, how about talking to him about *not* making us get up on those horses yet?"

"What is wrong with you?" Sam asked as she pulled away. "This is *so* not a big deal."

"It is to me," Seth mumbled. Putting his hand to his heart, he spoke to Sam in his sweetest, most endearing voice. "Please, Sammy-girl. Please tell Blu you'd rather we didn't do any acting on horseback yet. He'll understand – you being a newbie actor and all. Would you do this for me, please?"

Sam sighed and seriously considered Seth's request for a couple of seconds before looking him straight in the eye and saying, "No."

Seth grabbed Sam's elbow to pull her in so close his nose was practically inside her head. "You *have* to do this for me," he whispered.

Stunned, Sam asked, "Why?"

"Because I can't ride!" he hissed.

She pulled back. "Are you *kidding* me?" she asked in disbelief.

"Shhhh!" Seth pulled her closer again. "Keep it down!"

"Seth," she hissed, "this show takes place at a *stable*. It's called *Stable Stories*. Your character is a rich kid whose family expects him to win an Olympic medal in riding! You told me you knew how to ride!"

"No," Seth wagged a finger at her, "I never said I knew how to ride a horse. I said it would be great getting to spend time riding together, and once I learn – it will be."

Sam glared at him. "Did you pull that on Mr. Victorio too? He'd *never* have hired you if he'd known you couldn't ride!"

"Get over yourself," Seth sniped. "Any fool can learn to ride a horse, but it takes *talent* to be an actor. You need me way more than I need you."

Sam was seething inside, but that anger quickly turned to amusement as she watched Seth attempting to climb on to his horse. At first, he was standing too far back. Then he stepped closer and tried to put the wrong foot into the stirrups. Next he reached for the blanket under the saddle to pull himself up, and practically pulled the entire saddle down on his head. Lucky for him, one of the horse wranglers, who was assigned to help with the horses, noticed he was having problems and came to his rescue.

Waiting until she was sure he was watching, Sam gracefully slipped one foot into a stirrup, hopped, grabbed the saddle horn, and placed herself in the saddle perfectly. She reached out and scratched her horse behind his ears. "Easy there, big guy. I'll take care of you."

Seth shot her a seriously snotty glower. "Talking to your horsie? That's adorable."

Patting her horse's neck, Sam replied plainly, "No, it's what you do. This is Pumpkin. You are riding Ghost. I'd say hello to her if I were you."

Seth rolled his eyes before turning on that famous smile and calling out to Blu, "Okay, Mr. Director. Let's do this."

As he spoke, Seth inadvertently pulled up his heels so they touched Ghost's belly; that spooked the horse enough to make her tighten up and pull back. The tiny movement frightened Seth and he lunged forward, wrapping his arms around Ghost's neck. Now it was Sam's turn to roll her eyes.

"Places, everyone," Blu called out. He looked at the monitor attached to the camera. "Sam, I need you to move your horse closer to Seth and turn a bit to the left."

"How's this?" Sam effortlessly maneuvered Pumpkin as Blu had asked.

"Perfect!" he said. "Clear the set. This is a take." Blu pointed to the production assistant. "Call it."

Scurrying directly in front of the camera, the production assistant lifted a black and white bar attached to a large blackboard. "*Stable Stories*, scene one, take one." She slammed down the little bar, making a loud clacking noise.

Blu yelled, "Action!"

Seth, acting as his character, Graydon, looked into Sam's eyes adoringly.

"Kali," he said earnestly, "I don't care what my family thinks and I don't care what anybody says. You may be poor, but you are the classiest girl in the whole world."

"Gray," Sam replied with a shake of her head, "you say that now, but going out with me will cause you such grief that soon, it won't be worth it."

"You're worth it," Seth answered.

"Cut!" Blu yelled. "Seth, the line is *you are* worth it, not *you're* worth it. Your character speaks perfect English. No contractions. Let's do it again. Sam – excellent work! I like that little shake of the head. Be sure you keep that."

As everyone got ready for a second take, Sam did everything she could not to acknowledge Seth. She was completely disgusted with him. She wanted to race over and tell Mr. Victorio that Seth was a jerk who'd lied about being sick and knowing how to ride, but then she saw her mom watching the filming with such cavity-producing sickeningly sweet pride that she knew she couldn't do anything to ruin the shoot.

"You're doing great, honey!" Rose shouted.

"Rock star great!" Olga, standing next to Rose, joined in.

Carlos, on the other side of Olga, held up a piece of paper and a pen. "I get the first autograph when you finish," he called out.

"That's cute," Seth snorted.

"I love you, Seth!" Inga shouted, wildly waving her sign from the other side of the set.

Seth waved to Inga while speaking through gritted teeth: "At least one member of that family gets me."

The production assistant clicked the clacker again, and Blu shouted, "Action."

The scene started well, but a bird flew by and startled Seth, so he messed up his last line again. This type of thing happened over and over again, until they reached take number twelve, and everything finally came together.

"Are we done?" Sam asked. "I never thought one scene could take so long."

"This is nothing," Seth sneered. "If you can't handle the first scene, how do you think you're going to make it through an entire season?"

"Hush up, snarky," Sam snapped, "if you can't say anything nice, zip your lips, and leave me alone."

Stunned, Seth sat still with his mouth wide open. Sam wondered if she should warn him that you shouldn't do that around horses because a fly could wander in. Before she could say a word, she saw Mr. Victorio stride over and whisper something to Blu, who nodded. They called over the show's head writer, a young man named Everest, and the three pow-wowed for a few minutes before Blu and Everest walked onto the set.

"Seth, Sam," Blu said, "I've been chatting with Everest here and he's made a good point about this scene."

The young man pointed to a page in his script. "Originally, we had you both *almost* kissing at the end of another scene, but we've done a couple of rewrites, and now it makes more sense that you would here."

"Would what?" Sam asked.

"Kiss," Everest answered.

Kiss. Kiss Seth? *Kiss Seth!*

They expected her to kiss Seth – right there – in front of all those people! Her jaw fell open and a fly flew into *her* mouth. She gagged and spat to get it out. Sam's head throbbed as if it were about explode. Her heart raced so fast she got super-dizzy; she grabbed onto the saddle horn to stop herself from falling off Pumpkin. Her brain was screaming, *My first kiss can't be with Seth! No, no, no!*

CHAPTER 15

Blu saw Sam turn green, gag, and struggle to get the fly out of her mouth. "Sam?" He ran over and reached up to pat her on the back while yelling, "Someone get a bottle of water!"

The production assistant rushed over with a bottle. Sam slugged it down.

"You want to get down from Pumpkin?" Blu asked. "You need a minute to pull yourself together?"

"Blu," Sam panted, "I can't do this." She leaned down to speak privately to him. "Please don't make me kiss Seth! Not in front of all these people! I'm begging you! Please don't make me do this!"

Looking at her sympathetically, Blu softly explained, "I'm sorry, Sam, but we need it for the show. It makes sense for the story; it's only a little peck. There's no need to get worked up or be embarrassed. You *can* do it."

Shaking her head, she pleaded, "I can't! I just can't. You don't understand." She glanced over at Carlos. "It's...it's *complicated*. This'll be my *first kiss* and my first kiss has to be perfect! It *can't* be a throwaway! Maybe it's not the same for a guy as it is for a girl, but believe me – I'll be scarred for life! *Really! Please*, don't make me do this!"

"Sam," Blu said seriously, "as your director, I'm telling you that this is what the scene needs. As your friend, I'm promising you that this won't be a big deal. This is the reality of show business, it's a *business* and *your job* is to do what's in the script; it isn't always fun and sometimes we have to do things we'd rather not." He reached over to give Pumpkin a rub on the nose. "Now, let's get this in one take so everyone can break for lunch and be done with it."

Sam cringed. How could she force herself to kiss a creep she couldn't stand with the guy she was *so* totally into watching? Her first kiss *couldn't* be like this.

"Places!" Blu shouted as he headed back to his seat. "We've got the dialogue; let's pick it up with the kiss."

Out of the corner of her eye, Sam saw her mom's surprised reaction to the word, *kiss*. Rose turned angrily to Robert, who seemed to be doing his best to calm her down. Carlos and Olga both stood quietly, but with extremely confused expressions.

"Seth," Blu called out. "I need you to reach out and lift Sam's chin. Then you both lean in for a quick kiss. This is nothing mushy, just a simple smooch. Got it?"

Sam, still holding on to the saddle horn to try to stop the horrible spinning feeling, forced herself to nod while Seth yelled out, "Got it!"

The production assistant returned and called out, "*Stable Stories*, scene one B, take one." Again, she slammed down the bar, and made the clacking noise.

Blu shouted, "Action!"

While one hand gripped his saddle horn, Seth slowly reached out with the other. The shift of his weight made Ghost shift her weight as well and Seth panicked. He dropped his hand from Sam, hunkered down his whole body and froze with fear. Everyone on the set laughed, except for Sam, who remained stone still, trapped by her own dread.

Trying to appear brave, Seth laughed along with everyone else and called out, "Sorry, no problem, let's keep going."

Blu nodded. "We're still rolling, people," he yelled. "Focus, please."

Seth sat back up and began again. His one hand had a hardcore death-grip on the saddle horn, but he managed slowly to reach out and touch Sam's chin with the other. He brought her gaze up to meet his, and peered deep into her eyes. Sam gasped for air. *This is really going happen*, she thought. *I'm going to kiss Seth! I'm going to kiss Seth Black and then barf all over him!*

Seth leaned in toward Sam and she followed suit, but then, as they got close enough for her to feel his breath on her cheek, her whole body jerked back involuntarily. The movement was sudden and huge! It totally spooked Pumpkin; he reared up, kicking his front hooves into the air. Sam felt herself slipping backward. Everything seemed to be happening in slow motion. *This is bad*, she thought, but being an experienced rider, she knew the best thing to do was to throw herself off the back and roll away as fast as she could. She did so easily.

Unfortunately, Ghost was completely freaked by all the action and she too reared back with her hooves high in the sky. Seth threw his body forward and clung to the saddle horn for dear life.

"Stop, you stupid horse!" he screamed. "Stop!"

Desperate to hold on, Seth dug his heels into Ghost's side, not realizing this was the signal for the horse to go forward. The poor terrified animal took off like a shot! She raced off the set and down into the pasture with Seth on her back, shrieking like a little kid whose ice-cream cone had just been stolen.

No one moved – except for Inga. Waving her pink sign wildly, she ran down into the pasture, yelling out how much she loved Seth and promising to help him.

Still lying on the ground, Sam watched Seth gallop away, feeling badly – for *Ghost*.

Blu ran to Sam's side. "Are you okay?" he asked with real fear in his eyes.

Sam nodded. She began to giggle. "I'm fine. I'm fine...it's just...just that..." Her giggle turned into a major sob-fest. "Oh, Blu," she cried, "I don't want to do this. I *can't* do this!"

"All right," he sighed, "I'll pull the kiss. We'll figure something out."

Sam shook her head so hard that drippy mascara flew into the air, "No, not the kiss, *all* of it. I'm sorry. I'm so sorry. I can't imagine living this life another day and I don't know what to do because I want you and Michi and Lou to have jobs, I want my mom to keep her house and never have to worry about money or finding work, I want her to be proud of me, but I'm *miserable!*"

Unaware of her mom standing next to Blu, Sam jumped when she heard Rose exclaim, "Is *that* what this is about, Little Bit – the crew, the money, the *house*? Is *this* why you wanted to do the show? Did you think with Danni retiring we'd be *broke*?"

A sobbing, messy Sam whimpered, "Broke and homeless."

Rose handed her daughter a tissue. "I'll be right with you, Samantha." Then she turned and poked Robert square in the chest. "I knew it!" she barked. "I knew she didn't want to do the show! When will I learn not to listen to you?"

Everyone froze, except for Sam who began to giggle again. This time the giggles turned into gales of laughter. "No, Mom," she gasped, "Robert didn't talk me into anything. I didn't want you to have to move out of the house. You love it. With Danni quitting and moving out and everything changing so fast, I thought it was my turn to take care of you like you've always taken care of me. It was tough enough for you when Dad died, but you made it okay because you worked so hard, but now you're old and it won't be easy to find another job and move back into a tiny apartment and—"

"Hold on—" Rose studied her daughter carefully. "Did you just call me *old*?"

Sam shook her head. "I don't mean *old* old, just old*er*. Everything is changing so fast and it's a big stress to deal with change when you are older and alone and—"

Rose threw her arms in the air. "Older and *alone*? Where is this stuff coming from? Was that what the crazy dinner with Mr. Daniels was all about?"

Sam nodded, but her laughter turned back into tears.

"I'm so sorry, Mom! I'm so sorry! I thought I could do it. I thought I could save our house and make sure you didn't have to work, but I *can't*. I can't do the show! It's too much! Too much! I can't stand the rehearsals, the interviews, the makeup, the public appearances, and..." she took in a huge breath of air and let out a mighty wail, "and Seth is such a *butthead*!"

"Samantha," Rose replied sternly, "I've spoken to you before about such language."

"No, Rose," Mr. Victorio walked over. "She is correct. Seth is a butthead." He looked down at Sam while tapping a tiny hearing device wrapped around his ear. "I heard everything on that mike pack you're wearing. Yes, he *did* lie to me about knowing how to ride. I'm done trying to work with that ego." Nodding to Blu, he continued, "Your suspicion that he wasn't really sick this past week was correct." Mr. V held up his Blackberry. "A friend of mine in Canada e-mailed me a website with an article about *our boy* and how he was out on the town all the while he was crying to us about being at death's door." Turning to Olga, he pulled her in to give her a hug. "And *you* were absolutely right about him from day one. I am sorry

I didn't listen." He snapped his fingers. "What is it you call him?"

"A twerp," she said with a definitive nod.

"Ahh, yes." Mr. V looked down at Sam again. "That twerp is *fired*!"

Sam breathed a sigh of relief before launching into a major apology for ruining the show, but Mr. V wouldn't hear it. "Do not worry about a thing," he said. "I can find another actress to replace you. Of course, you are a very special girl, but there are a million young actresses who really do want this life and the concept for this show is great. Your friends will still have work. I need a week to replace both you and…" He looked over at Olga.

"The twerp," Olga, Carlos, and Sam all said at the same time.

Mr. V nodded again. "Yes. Better you quit now, before we've done too much actual filming, than you try to survive a year and we lose everything. You shouldn't feel guilty. *Stable Stories* will miss you, but we'll all be fine."

Sam was the happiest she'd been in a very long time. She leaped to her feet and hugged Mr. Victorio.

"Thank you, thank you, thank you!" she half laughed, half cried.

"Hey there," Olga joked, "release my dad."

Sam let go of Mr. V and threw her arms around Olga. "I'm free!" she cried. "I'm free! We—" She stopped mid-sentence. "But the *house*!" She turned to Rose. "Oh, Mom, I'm so sorry! By quitting *Stable Stories*, I've just killed *The Devine Life*, haven't I?"

"In essence, yes," Rose replied. "But it's not as bad as you're making it out to be. I told you I'd saved plenty of money the past couple of years. When we initially thought we were losing the show because Danni was quitting, I began discussions with the producers about buying the house. They were more than happy to have a willing buyer. They don't need the hassle of maintaining a house that's no longer a business expense. Trust me, we may not be chartering anymore private jets for a while, but we can keep the house and not have to worry about money. Your *old* mom has become quite the businesswoman. I've got it all covered."

Sam hugged her mom with all her might before whipping back to Olga. "It really is all good! We can go riding again and talk on the phone and hang out and go to school and get in trouble for passing notes and texting each other instead of paying attention, just like we used to! Won't that be the best?"

Olga beamed with joy. "The very best!" She started to sniff. "It's been unbearable not being able to talk to you. No, it was beyond that! It was *gut-busting* awful! You're my best friend! I'd say you were like my own sister, except my own sister is such a *blech*!"

That made Sam laugh again.

Blu turned to the crew. "That's a wrap for today, everyone. You'll all get an e-mail with updates. We'll be shutting down production for no more than a week. Don't go taking any other jobs. You're all still gainfully employed. Oh, and would somebody please go and track down Seth and his horse. Remember, we need to take care of all the valued members of our TV family, so please, when they return, be extra kind to *Ghost*."

The whole crew applauded.

"Sam," Blu said kindly, "you are officially released from this set and this show."

Sam's eyes welled up with tears again. Blu reached over and gave her a hug. "Be cool. We'll talk at your sister's concert." Letting go, he gave her a gentle nudge toward Carlos. "Carlos?" he asked. "Would you please escort Ms. Devine to her trailer?"

Sam blushed from head to toe as Carlos held out his hand for her. Neither one spoke as they walked. Once they reached Sam's trailer, they both stood silently.

"I'll see you at Danni's concert?" he asked.

"Oh, big *yes!*" Sam smiled. "I can't wait! Danni worked so hard to make sure this performance would be perfect, and now that I understand a little about how tough it is to be a performer, I'm more proud of her than I ever thought I could be."

Carlos nodded. "That's funny, I was going to say the very same thing about you."

As Sam looked up to smile at Carlos, he bent down and gave Sam the softest little kiss on the lips anyone could ever imagine. Then, grinning broadly, he walked away. Sam melted down onto the step of her trailer. *Her first kiss!* She got her first kiss – from the guy she liked – and it was better than she ever dreamed it could be. There was no drama, no trauma, no shenanigans. It was a totally perfect moment.

Floating on a cloud, Sam drifted inside her trailer.

Nothing could ruin this feeling, she thought. And then she caught sight of herself in the mirror. Huge streaks of black mascara had run down her face, her hair was wild and crazy, her eyes were red and puffy; she looked like a rabid zebra. "Wow," she said out loud. "He must really like me – *like me,* like me!"

CHAPTER 16

Click click click, clack clack click.

I've had good days. I've had great days. Yesterday, my first (and *last*) day of shooting *Stable Stories*, started out award-winningly awful, but it turned out to be one of the best days of my entire life! *For reals!!*

Long story short — I'm free!!! No more TV, no more rehearsals, no more interviews, and NO MORE *SETH*!!!

Yesterday could have been a total disaster, but Mom came through in a serious way. After I totally ruined my first (and *last*) day of shooting (with more than a little help from Seth – who shall now forever be called *The Liar King*), Mom came into my trailer and we had a major heart-to-heart. Seems she truly has saved up a lot of money and she spoke to the production guys from *The Devine Life* and *we are staying in our house*! The details are boring, but basically Mom cut a killer deal and *we* are buying this place! How cool is that?

But wait – there's more! Robert had already spoken to Mom about becoming the manager for this new pop-singing dude he's going to start agenting. Mom loves the idea! I feel like such a doofus: *all* my worries about her having to find a job to support our family were for nothing. Pretty ironic, don't ya think? Maybe I need to be better at sharing my thoughts with my mom before I devise my next major plan to *save-the-day*? MAYBE (tee hee).

Danni's farewell concert last night was *the most amazing show* EVER! It wasn't huge – only around 100 people, but Robert had coughed up his own money to buy tickets and sodas and snacks for all the *STARS* kids and volunteers, so the charity got a large donation and Danni made up for the previous fiasco. Also, it wasn't a crazy, fancy concert; there weren't a bunch of dancers or a billion costume changes. It was just her and her band singing and playing (yes – Danni really DID play one song on the guitar this time and she was *awesome*). It was as if her heart was finally back in her music. It sounded the way it used to be before she became a big pop star. Who knows, maybe after a year or two of college, she'll miss performing and want to come back... or maybe she'll become a music teacher. That would be cool! Either way, I'm really proud of her.

Get this, just before the final number, Danni starts talking about the end of her career as a pop singer and the end of *The Devine Life* reality show and how happy she is to be doing her last show for her friend Rowan and the *STARS* charity, to finally fulfil that promise of playing the guitar live. But then she says there is one other promise she needs to keep.

Blu and Robert then lifted ME out of the audience and carried ME onstage where Danni had a HUGE chocolate-chip cookie-dough ice-cream cake with fourteen candles wheeled out! For ME! She explained that my b-day was coming up and this would be her last opportunity to do something majorly embarrassing for me (she was right about that!) so she got the whole audience to sing "Happy Birthday." Have you ever had a hundred people sing "Happy Birthday" to you? It's wickedly fun!

After shoving a seriously embarrassing hunk of ice-cream cake in my mouth, I licked my hand to clean it, and my tongue hit Olga's silver rose ring (you better believe I'd put it back on the first chance I got). That reminded me that I still had

Seth's…er…I mean, *The Liar King's*, ring in my pocket. I quietly slipped it to Danni and told her to give it to Rowan later as a friendship ring. I didn't see the actual *gifting*, but I heard a crazy loud, squealy "thank you" backstage and saw Rowan hugging Danni, so I'm guessing the present was a hit.

So that was my day: got let go from my TV show, had a huge crowd sing "Happy Birthday" to me, my sis gave the greatest performance of her life, my mom has a wonderful job and we get to stay in our mansion that Mom loves more than a French fry loves ketchup!

Nothing else could have possibly made that day any better…except for maybe…*the PERFECT FIRST KISS!*

Which I also got yesterday!

Oh yeah! That's right!

But a lady doesn't kiss and tell, so I'm not going to discuss that any further. Except to say: HOORAY!!!!!!!!!!!!!!!!!!!!!!!!!!!!!!!!!!!!!!! (x4ever)

I have to go now. Olga and Carlos are bringing a pizza for dinner so we can chow down while watching videos as we wait for the movers to finish the packing for Danni. Yup — last night was our final night with our little family unit sleeping under one roof. I asked Olga and Carlos to be here tonight for Danni's final farewell because I'm afraid I may lose it when I realize my big sister is officially out-of-the-house. Not that I'm worried this will happen any time soon, the movers *are still* trying to get all her boxes into the truck (and it's an *enormous* truck, my sister has a *lot* of shoes).

But before I go, I need to give a major shout out to somebody very special. I can't say his name, but his favorite color is *blu*.
8-)

To this special friend – I miss you already. Thank you for being the best pseudo big brother a girl could ever hope to have. I can't believe you gave up your "new" job to leave town for a whole year and direct a documentary on polar bears. Don't forget to "tweet" me if you meet Santa up there at the North Pole (rotfl).

And in another moment of true awesomeness, this special friend convinced Mr. V and Robert to replace him with *co-directors* for *Stable Stories*. Break a leg, Michi & Lou!!! I can't wait to watch your show!

@> (that's the symbol for a bouquet of roses)

I just heard the doorbell ding – that's Olga and Carlos with the pizza! Time for me, Sam – the non-acting, non-reality TV-show star little sister of a former pop star – to go chow down!

Bye for now.

Rather than watching a movie, Carlos suggested they plug Sam's laptop into the TV and watch some of those old Muppet videos online that Sam had mentioned. The three friends had a blast singing along to the songs and cracking up at the silly skits and corny jokes. When Olga went into the kitchen to grab more soda, Carlos turned to Sam and handed her a little box.

Sam's eyes grew huge.

"You can relax," Carlos laughed, "it's not a ring."

Giggling, Sam opened the box and was thrilled to find a tiny frog bracelet.

"It's not Kermit," he said quietly, "but I thought it might make you smile anyway. You don't have to wear it. It's only a small thing to remember a day when you found the courage to do a very big thing."

"I love it. I really love it! I want to wear it right now," Sam said, but then she shook her head. "I'd hardly call falling off my horse a big thing."

"No," Carlos said as he pulled out the bracelet and put it around Sam's wrist. "But admitting to everyone that you were unhappy, being true to what was inside your heart – that took more strength than anything

I've ever seen anyone do."

Softly, Sam replied, "Thank you," she smiled, "ya big *cheese-toe*."

"*Chistoso!*" he laughed.

He leaned toward Sam. *Yes!* she thought excitedly. *Here comes perfect kiss number two!* She began to lean in as well, but just then Olga burst back into the room.

"Come on, guys!" she called out. "The truck is packed. Danni is standing in the driveway waiting to say goodbye."

Carlos and Sam exchanged a very silly look before standing up and heading to the front door.

As they stepped outside, they found Rose with her arms wrapped around her eldest daughter.

"I'm going to miss you so much," she said tearfully. "I can't believe my baby is moving out!"

"Mom," Danni whined, "I'm not a baby. I'm a phone call away. Come on, don't make this any harder than it already is."

Sniffing back her sobs, Rose patted Danni on the back as she slowly released her from her bear hug. "Okay, okay." She planted one last sloppy kiss on her daughter's cheek before stepping back.

With her lower lip quivering, Sam gave her sister a tiny, weak wave.

Danni threw her arms out wide. "Get over here!"

Sam ran over and gave Danni the biggest hug ever.

"You know how much I'm going to miss seeing you every morning?" Danni whispered.

"Almost as much as I'm going to miss your snoring every night," Sam replied as she wiped her damp eyes on her sister's shirt.

The two girls giggled and gave each other friendly slugs on the arm. They stood there staring at one another until Sam said, "Go on. Get out of here! I'm tired of looking at your ugly mug."

Danni grinned. "Back at ya, Little Bit." Then she hopped into her sports car and slowly drove down the driveway.

The truck followed close behind. They reached the street, turned right, drove about fifteen yards, turned into the very next driveway, and drove up to the house next door.

Sam ran as fast as she could across her front lawn,

hurdling the small hedge that separated the two homes, hopped up the front steps, and planted herself squarely in front of the door.

As Danni stepped out of her car, Sam threw her arms wide open.

"Let me be the first to officially welcome you to your new home!" she yelled with glee. "Say hello to Casa Devine Duo! I hope you'll be very happy here, but I have to warn you," she put a hand up to her mouth and pretended to be sharing something very top secret, "I hear the neighbors are nice, but a little *eccentric*."

Catch up with Sam's
fabulously funny blog in...

MY SISTER'S A POP STAR

Hi, I'm Sam, welcome to my blog!

Guess what? My sister Danni is
THE number-one, superstar pop princess –
and my life's totally crazy!
I can't wait for Danni's world tour to end so
we can get to be a normal family again.

Well, as normal as you can be with Danni's
slimeball agent hanging around.
I definitely think he's up to something – and I
have a sneaky feeling I'm not gonna like it...

*Backstage passes, private jets and
TV stardom – life's one mega-rockin' rollercoaster
when your sister's a pop star.*

ISBN: 9780794528997

Join Sam for another
crazy celeb escapade in...

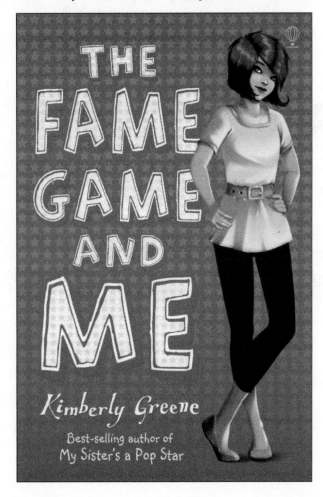

THE
FAME
GAME
AND
ME

Kimberly Greene

Best-selling author of
My Sister's a Pop Star

THE FAME GAME AND ME

Hi, I'm Sam, welcome to my blog!

Some people dream of being famous.
Well, I am – and it's a *total nightmare!*
My sister, Danni, is a big-time
POP PRINCESS, so I spend most of
my life trying to figure out the rules to
this freaky FAME GAME!

Danni's discovered it's tough
at the top since a rival pop-diva starting
competing for the #1 spot. And
I've just found out an AMAZING secret
about our family. I only hope our life
in the limelight won't make things
even CRAZIER – but I guess
that's showbiz, right?

ISBN: 9780794529000

A few things you didn't know about KIMBERLY GREENE

☆ Which five words would you use to describe yourself?

☆ Busy
☆ Chocoholic
☆ Funny
☆ Devilish
☆ Relentless

☆ How do you spend a typical day?

Every day is different, but I always get my morning started by walking down to the local Coffee Bean & Tea Leaf for breakfast with my family and friends.

Once I've finished my beloved Blueberry-Pomegranate Tea Latte (no sugar added – natch!) and got my two-year-old to stop yapping and eat his banana, we head home, stopping only to say hello to EVERY SINGLE human and puppy dog we encounter along the way (sigh). Once we get back home, I'm insanely busy with meetings, doing research, creating presentations, materials and movies for my fellow professors and our graduate students (yup, I'm a teacher – of teachers). I am on my computer at least eight hours a day. I have a special file on my laptop where I keep a running list of future book ideas and I find myself adding all kinds of little thoughts or funny character quirks to it almost every day. These days, many of my ideas come from stuff my little boy has said or done; having a two-year-old with the vocabulary of a ten-year-old is crazy entertaining!

☆ How do you write?

I think *a lot* before I write. I try to "see" each "scene" of a story in my head and then replay it with small changes to ensure each word that goes into the book is worth reading.

⭐ What is your ideal way to spend a day off?

SKIING!!!!!!!!!!!!!!!!!!!!!!!!!!!!!!

If skiing isn't an option (which it isn't very often these days), then any day where I can be with my family, walking along the beach or playing in the backyard, is better than anything.

Although, I do miss riding my motorcycle; I have to find more time for that.

⭐ What would you be if you weren't a writer?

I've been writing stories since I was eight years old. Getting my work published has truly been a dream come true, but honestly, even if I hadn't achieved this goal – I'd still be writing.

⭐ What's on your iPod?

These days I have mostly movies and photos taking up ALL the space on my iPod. My little boy has given me the opportunity to revisit all kinds of movies and music I loved when I was a kid.